//////// NASCAR®

SECRETS and LEGENDS

HITTING THE BRAKES
by Ken Casper

From the opening green flag at Daytona to the final checkered flag at Homestead, the competition will be fierce for the NASCAR Sprint Cup Series championship.

The **Grosso** family practically has engine oil in their veins. For them racing represents not just a way of life but a tradition that goes back to NASCAR's inception. Like all families, they also have a few skeletons to hide. What happens when someone peeks inside the closet becomes a matter that threatens to destroy them.

The **Murphys** have been supporting drivers in the pits for generations, despite a vendetta with the Grossos that's almost as old as NASCAR itself! But the Murphys have their own secrets... and a few indiscretions that could cost them everything.

The **Branches** are newcomers, and some would say upstarts. But as this affluent Texas family is further enmeshed in the world of NASCAR, they become just as embroiled in the intrigues on and off the track.

The **Motor Media Group** are the PR people responsible for the positive public perception of NASCAR's stars. They are the glue that repairs the damage. And more than anything, they feel the brunt of the backlash....

These NASCAR families have secrets to hide, and reputations to protect. This season will test them all.

Dear Reader,

Writing is a solitary business. Most of the time the only companions you have are the characters you're creating in your book—and sometimes all they want to do is play bumper cars with your brain and be generally uncooperative.

Then one day I was invited to write a NASCAR story as part of this continuity. Like a fan in the grandstands, I wouldn't be alone anymore! It could have been a disaster, of course. Rather than arguing with my characters, I could have found myself caught up in a writers' family feud. Not a chance. I was teamed up with a bunch of other NASCAR fanatics who, like a teammate offering a draft, were happy to share their characters, their ideas and their incredible knowledge of things NASCAR as we raced toward the checkered flag.

I hope you enjoy the results of our collaboration as much as I've enjoyed contributing to it.

Ken Casper

NASCAR

HITTING THE BRAKES

Ken Casper

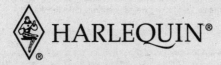

HARLEQUIN®

TORONTO • NEW YORK • LONDON
AMSTERDAM • PARIS • SYDNEY • HAMBURG
STOCKHOLM • ATHENS • TOKYO • MILAN • MADRID
PRAGUE • WARSAW • BUDAPEST • AUCKLAND

ISBN-13: 978-0-373-21791-5
ISBN-10:   0-373-21791-9

HITTING THE BRAKES

Copyright © 2008 by Harlequin Books S.A.

Kenneth Casper is acknowledged as the author of this work.

NASCAR® and the NASCAR Library Collection are registered trademarks of the National Association for Stock Car Auto Racing, Inc.

KEN CASPER,

aka K.N. Casper, figures his writing career started back in the sixth grade when a teacher ordered him to write a "theme" explaining his misbehavior over the previous semester. To his teacher's chagrin, he enjoyed stringing just the right words together to justify his less-than-stellar performance. That's not to say he's been telling tall tales to get out of scrapes ever since, but…

Born and raised in New York City, Ken is now a transplanted Texan. He and Mary, his wife of thirty-plus years, own a horse farm in San Angelo. Along with their two dogs, six cats and eight horses—at last count!—they also board and breed horses and Mary teaches English riding. She's a therapeutic riding instructor for the handicapped, as well.

Life is never dull. Their two granddaughters visit several times a year and feel right at home with the Casper menagerie. Grandpa and Mimi do everything they can to make sure their visits will be lifelong fond memories. After all, isn't that what grandparents are for?

You can keep up with Ken and his books on his Web site at www.kencasper.com.

To the other writers in this series:
From the new girl at the track
to the seasoned expert, and all the dedicated fans
in between, you've been inspirations.
Thank you!

The scandal surrounding the Branch family continues to take a toll on NASCAR drivers Bart and Will Branch, who are struggling to make the cut for the Chase for the NASCAR Sprint Cup. To make matters worse, the sudden illness of Bart's team owner Richard Latimer has everyone nervous about the fate of PDQ Racing.

PROLOGUE

CHARLOTTE DAILY HERALD
PDQ Racing Team Owner Hospitalized
CHARLOTTE, N.C.—Motor Media Group public relations spokesperson, Anita Wolcott, today issued a statement that following the NASCAR Sprint Cup series race in Charlotte on Sunday, Richard Latimer, owner of PDQ Racing, was rushed to the hospital by ambulance. Wolcott failed to identify the specific health condition that prompted the well-known team owner's emergency hospitalization, and a spokesperson at Charlotte General has refused to discuss details about the patient's medical condition or history, except to say that he is in stable condition and resting comfortably.

Richard Latimer, 73, millionaire businessman and noted philanthropist, established PDQ Racing almost twenty years ago, following his retirement as a successful commodities trader. Since then he's devoted most of his energy to NASCAR, where for years he ran three highly successful teams in the NASCAR Nationwide Series. Last year he moved into the NASCAR Sprint Cup Series with Bart Branch, whose brother, Will, joined Taney Motorsports at the same time. Competition between the charismatic bachelors immediately appealed to fans, but spectator interest in the twins went up meteorically three months ago when their father, Branch Mutual Trust president Hilton Branch, suddenly disappeared without a trace. Early speculation revolved around the possibility that the powerful executive had been kidnapped by terrorists for ransom or that he was murdered. A mandatory audit of the huge banking conglomerate's financial records, however, subsequently disclosed that a large sum of money—estimates run as high as a quarter-billion dollars—was also missing. Since then, Hilton Branch has been sought by authorities, not as a probable victim of foul play, but as the perpetrator of one of the largest individual banking embezzlement cases in U.S. history.

What effect the sudden illness of Richard Latimer will have on PDQ Racing or its involvement in the NASCAR Sprint Cup Series is unclear. The scion of an old, prominent Southern family, he never married. Who might take over management of the racing team, if he is no longer able to do so himself, remains unclear.

CHAPTER ONE

IT WAS THE SMELL THAT HIT her first. Alcohol floating above a thin miasma of pine scent and an indefinable mustiness. Her stomach did a momentary heave and settled as the automatic doors hissed closed behind her. She hated hospitals.

"Richard Latimer," she told the silver-haired volunteer behind the receptionist's counter.

The woman fumbled through a sheaf of curly-edged papers. "Room 618. Elevators are down the corridor to your right and then left."

Anita didn't have to make a conscious effort to process the information. She knew the way. All too well. "Thank you."

The private room on the sixth floor was large and dimly lit. Electronic monitors beeped rhythmically. Intravenous tubing coiled down from clear plastic bags of fluids. Richard was a large man, but he looked small under the white sheet and fawn-colored knitted blanket. The head of the bed was raised, its occupant pasty-faced and slack-jawed.

Anita stepped closer, stood by the bed and studied him a few seconds, before adding her modest bouquet to the side table already crammed with much more impressive displays, then she slipped her hand into his.

"Hello, Richard. It's Anita. I just came by to see how you're doing."

No response, either in his expression or his touch. From experience, she knew that didn't necessarily mean he hadn't heard her.

"Everyone's pulling for you, Richard. You'll be up and around in no time. Just hang in there. We're all praying for you."

She stood there another minute, maybe two, before she released his dry, limp hand. Still gazing at him, she turned absently away and collided hard with a warm, solid body.

"I'm sorry," the man said in a deep voice, his hands quickly bracketing her upper arms. "I didn't mean to startle you."

Her heart pounded painfully for several beats. "I…I—"

She was completely, angrily unnerved. Whether it was merely because of his unexpected presence, her sudden, overwhelming sense of helplessness or something about the man himself, she wasn't sure.

"Are you all right?" His eyes—they seemed black in this shadowy light—peered at her with concern.

She forced herself to relax her adrenaline-spiked muscles and reposition her feet enough to regain her balance. "I didn't know you were here," she half mumbled, half accused.

He removed his hands and took a step back and to the side. "Again, my apologies. You were talking to Uncle Richard when I came in, but I thought you'd heard me enter."

"Uncle?"

He motioned her to the door, reached forward to open it. As he did so, she couldn't help notice the sinewy contour of his forearm below the short-sleeve white cotton shirt. She stepped into the hallway, then spun around to face him. He pulled the door almost closed.

"I'm Jim Latimer," he said, coming forward and extending his hand.

Instinctively she took it. "Anita Wolcott. I'm—"

"The Motor Media Group public-relations rep for PDQ Racing."

"How did—"

"Uncle Richard has spoken about you. He's been very impressed with the way you've handled the Hilton Branch scandal."

Anita wasn't quite sure how to reply. She was, after all, just doing her job. But why had Richard been discussing her job performance with his nephew anyway?

"He's a wonderful man," she said, then quickly added, "Your uncle, I mean." She managed to crack a smile. "Not Hilton Branch."

Jim chuckled softly. "I'm glad you clarified that."

"How is he?" she asked.

The lightheartedness instantly vanished. Richard's nephew took a deep breath and exhaled. "Not good, I'm afraid."

A nurse came down the corridor pushing a square red cart with a multitude of little drawers and doors, almost a smaller version of the huge tool boxes that NASCAR teams used at the race tracks. In a sense, she supposed, it was. The woman stopped outside the patient's room, nodded to the visitors, checked the notes on a metal clipboard and went inside.

"There's nothing we can do here at the moment," Jim said. "If you have a few minutes, how about letting me buy you a cup of coffee? I've consumed a fair quantity of the house brew in the last two and a half days to vouch that it's reasonably palatable."

Anita hadn't planned on hanging around. A quick visit

to pay her respects, to see if there was anything she could do—there rarely was in situations like this—and be gone. But just then, her stomach emitted a loud, hollow grumble. She hadn't had lunch.

"And in spite of this being a hospital—" he smiled again "—the food isn't half bad, either."

Jim Latimer, she realized, was a very good-looking man. Close to six feet tall, he had broad compact shoulders and a deep chest that tapered down to a slim waist and narrow hips. He reminded her of a gymnast, though on a larger scale. Neatly trimmed thick ebony hair, just long enough to show a subtle wave. And eyes that, even out here in the afternoon sunlight that pored through the window behind her, were as dark as burnt umber.

"I'll fill you in on what I know about Uncle Richard's condition," he added.

RICHARD HAD SAID HIS NEW public-relations rep was a pretty gal. An understatement, if ever Jim had heard one. This woman, Anita Wolcott, was gorgeous. Golden-red hair, emerald-green eyes and a creamy soft complexion. She was conservatively dressed in a charcoal pinstripe pantsuit and lavender, wide-lapeled silk blouse. Not so conservative in cut, however, that he wasn't aware of her distinctively feminine curves. Simple gold studs in her ears, a braided gold chain around her neck. She was wearing an amethyst ring on her right hand, he noticed, but no jewelry on her left. Richard had casually mentioned she was single, probably hoping Jim would ask more about her.

They retraced their steps to the elevator and descended to the second floor. Since it was the middle of the afternoon, the cafeteria was nearly empty. Each poured a cup of coffee. Jim talked her into eating something. She chose a small chicken wrap. He opted for a piece of apple pie.

At the checkout he started to offer to pay, but she already had her wallet out of her purse. His uncle would undoubtedly have finessed picking up the tab "for the little lady," claiming it was the privilege of an old Southern gentleman. Jim didn't think he could get away with the same line. Instead she surprised him by paying for his coffee and pie before he had a chance to protest. He kept the chuckle that bubbled up to himself and thanked her.

She led him to a table against the far wall, where they sat opposite each other. When she put her back to the outside window and let him face the glare, he realized, not without a certain amusement, that she was a woman used to being in control of things.

He watched her peel the paper off her wrap, mesmerized by the feminine grace of her movements. Her glance told him she was aware of him studying her.

"You were right," she said, after taking a sip of her coffee. "This isn't bad at all."

"I'm glad you're enjoying it." He certainly was, observing her closely.

"You were going to tell me about your uncle."

HIS PLAYFUL GRIN FADED, his face grew solemn, double ridges appearing between his thick black eyebrows.

"He's had a massive stroke," he said. "They've been able to dissolve the clot on his brain with medication, but that was two days ago and he still hasn't regained consciousness. They did a CAT scan this morning. No more clots, but they can't say for sure how much damage might have been done, and they won't know till he comes around...if he comes around."

She ignored her food. "That bad?"

He nodded. "On the other hand, he may wake up and order a twenty-four-ounce porterhouse, medium rare, with baked potato, sour cream and bacon bits."

Anita did her best to match his upbeat attitude. With a forced smile, she said, "Somehow I don't think his doctor will approve that menu."

More by reflex than appetite, she took a bite of her food, her mind skittering between fond sentiments for the man in the sickbed upstairs and thoughts about the one sitting across from her.

"I've known Richard for only a few months, since the beginning of the season. He's never said much about his family. Since you share the same last name," she said, after another sip of coffee, "I assume you're his brother's son."

"His younger brother," Jim confirmed. "There are also two sisters. Uncle Richard is the eldest and the hero of the family, the one who made all the money and shared it with just about everybody."

"If you've been here for the past three days, you and he must be close," Anita observed. "What about your job? Can you afford to take time away from it?"

He grinned at her, clearly amused. "The boss won't mind." Each resumed eating. "I saw your press release in the paper this morning," he went on a minute later. "You handled those vultures very well."

"Thanks. I think. Am I right in concluding you don't hold the fourth estate in high regard?"

He shrugged. "I admit to having limited contact with

them, but on the few occasions when I have, or have been personally familiar with a story they've covered, I've never known them to get it right."

"Maybe they just didn't see the story the way you did. Has it ever occurred to you that *your* perspective may have been the one that was slanted?"

"Regarding opinions, maybe," he conceded, "but I bet we can look at half a dozen reports at random and find at least one factual error in each. There's no excuse for that, not from people who call themselves professionals."

A perfectionist? Or simply a man of high standards? She felt as if she'd just stepped into a minefield and wasn't quite sure how she'd gotten there—or how to get out.

"The overwhelming majority of people in the business," she said, "try very hard to do an honest job, but they're not computers. People do make mistakes. Unfortunate though that may be, most of their errors are inconsequential."

His continuing scowl made it clear he wasn't moved by her argument.

"The big question in this case," she said, trying to remain calm, "is what effect Richard's illness is going to have on PDQ Racing? From what I saw and what you've said, it doesn't seem likely he'll be manning the helm for a while. Who's in charge while he's sidelined? Do you know?"

Jim sighed discontentedly, the thin smile on his lips not one of happiness or glee. "You're looking at him."

CHAPTER TWO

A WOMAN WEARING GREEN hospital scrubs approached the table. "Mr. Latimer?"

He looked up, apprehension written in his expression. "Yes."

"Your uncle seems to be rousing. The doctor thought you might want to be there when he wakes up."

They immediately returned upstairs. Anita had a litany of questions to ask Jim, but this didn't seem the appropriate time. There would be other opportunities. As they stood in the elevator, side by side, in silence, their proximity and the isolation within the small cubicle made her all the more aware of his size, of the breadth of his shoulders. She glanced over at his hand, only a few inches from hers, remembered the feel of its grasp when she collided with him. Even now, she felt unbalanced, in need of his solid strength. Her pulse was tripping, she realized, when the door opened. A wave of heat ran through her when he half turned and motioned with his arm for her to precede him. Her insides fluttered. It wasn't the man before her that made her so edgy, she told herself. It was the place; she hated hospitals.

As it turned out, Richard hadn't actually regained consciousness, he'd only become restless.

"That's still a positive sign," the doctor on duty insisted.

But it didn't take more than a brief conversation with him to realize it might be hours, even days, before they could accurately evaluate the older man's condition.

While the physician continued to examine his patient and the nurse replenished the intravenous fluids, Jim motioned Anita back outside the room.

"Thanks for coming," he said once they were in the hallway. "But there's no need for you to hang around. I'm sure you have other things to do. I appreciate your coming by, and I know Uncle Richard will be pleased when I tell him you were here."

He reached into his back pocket for his wallet and took out a business card.

"Got a pen?" he asked.

She rummaged in her handbag, withdrew a ballpoint, clicked it and handed it to him. He cupped the card in the palm of his left hand—no ring, she noted—and scribbled on its back.

"The number on the front," he said, "will get you my answering service. Here's my personal cell number. If you have any questions—"

She examined the face of the card. James Latimer. Independent CPA. She understood now his frown when she'd made the crack about computers. But how was she to know? He didn't exactly match the stereotype of an accountant.

"I'll call you later to find out how he's doing," she said. "We'll need to prepare another press release. Keep the public informed."

The disapproving expression in his eyes didn't surprise her, but at least he didn't object.

"I could be here for hours," he said, "and since they don't

like people using mobile phones in the hospital, it might be better if I called you. What's your number?"

She rattled it off, then started diving into her purse again. "Let me give you my card. It has the number on it."

He smiled. "No need. I'll remember it." He repeated it back to her, then broadened his smile. "I'm an accountant, remember? Numbers are my racket, just like spin is yours."

He said it with a smile, so she assumed he was trying to be funny rather than insulting. She hoped so, especially if he was going to be taking over PDQ Racing.

"If there are any changes in his condition," she replied, "please let me know. Or if you need anything, don't hesitate to call. I really would like to help."

"Thanks," he said, sounding touched by the offer.

In her car a few minutes later, she thought about the two men she'd left. Miracles happened, and modern medicine was remarkable in what it could do with conditions that only a few years ago seemed hopeless. She just prayed it didn't take a miracle for Richard to recover.

As for the younger Latimer, he was something of a contradiction. Physically attractive, without a doubt. Intelligent and seemingly capable of charm. But there was an edge, as well, one that both irritated and intrigued her.

After turning off the main thoroughfare onto a more lightly traveled secondary road, she decided to check the voice mail on her cell phone. Half a dozen messages from reporters. She didn't have anything for them yet, and they'd no doubt be bugging her again, so she deleted them. That left three calls she really did have to answer. Sandra Jacobs, the head of Motor Media Group. Bart Branch, PDQ's sole driver in the NASCAR Sprint Cup Series. And Philip Whalen, his crew chief.

She dialed the boss first.

"How's Richard?" Sandra asked, the moment she recognized Anita's voice.

"Still comatose, I'm afraid, but he's starting to become restless. The doctor seems to think that's a good sign."

"They always say that." Sandra's tone wasn't cynical, just informative. "I've been getting a lot of calls from sponsors, team members and, of course, the media. Been using the usual lines—resting comfortably, still undergoing tests, et cetera, but they're not going to put up with those dodges much longer. The gossip and speculation are already running wild in the NASCAR grapevine. We need to come out with a new statement ASAP."

Anita agreed. "I ran into Richard's nephew at the hospital," she said. "Turns out he's the one who will be taking over PDQ, at least for the time being. I got his permission to put out a new press release."

"Good." Sandra paused for a moment. "I don't recall Richard ever saying anything about a nephew."

"I've never met him before, either. All I know about him, at the moment, is that he's an accountant."

"Hmm. That could be good or bad. How much does he know about NASCAR?"

"I can't say, at this point," Anita replied. "We didn't get a chance to talk for very long. I do know he isn't fond of the press."

Sandra chuckled. "That makes him one of millions."

Anita agreed again. Having a passive mistrust of reporters and journalists was healthy, but she'd gotten the feeling Jim Latimer had an active animus against the media, which was another matter altogether. Hostility bred hostility, and the last thing anybody in the public eye needed was an antagonistic press. On the other hand, it would be a mistake on her part to draw any conclusions based on such a brief conversation, especially in these circumstances.

"I need to call Bart, then Phil, and fill them in on Richard's status. I'll give them a heads-up that Jim will be assuming command, at least for a while."

"The faster we can get this information to the people who are directly affected, the better," Sandra concurred. "We don't want them hearing it on TV or reading about it on the Internet first. I sure hope Richard pulls through."

"Me, too," Anita said. "I'll prepare a news release from home tonight and forward it to you."

"Just go ahead and release it and send me a courtesy copy," her boss said casually, as if no real thought had gone into the decision. Its significance was not lost on Anita, however. She felt like a teenager who'd just been given the keys to the family car. Sandra Jacobs had every right to see press releases *before* they were issued.

"Will do," Anita said, "and thanks." She broke the connection.

Since she was now only five minutes from home, she decided to wait until she got there to make her other telephone calls. She wanted to spend the next few minutes savoring the vote of confidence she'd just received.

The house, a modest brick-and-stucco ranch, was quiet, of course. Not even the whir of her mother's oxygen generator was there to greet her anymore. She'd lived here most of her life, her parents having bought it when she was six years old. Four years later, her father was killed in a freak accident at the construction site where he was working.

She remembered him fondly, the big strong man she ran to every evening, the man who gathered her up in his arms, whirled her around and wanted to know all about her day. He'd smelled of pine lumber and concrete dust. Probably of sweat, too, but she didn't remember that. He would always be the symbol of a happy childhood. The ideal daddy.

Her mother coped as well as any young grieving widow and parent could. Anita had no complaints, but then when she was fifteen, Virginia was diagnosed with multiple sclerosis, and life took another detour.

She flipped the kitchen light switch and the recessed fluorescent fixture flickered and buzzed.

"I really ought to sell this house," she mumbled to herself. "Rent an apartment, buy a town house or a condo. A place I don't have to maintain, where I can just call someone to change an inconvenient light bulb or oil a squeaky hinge."

But if she did that, wouldn't she be losing even another dimension of her life—the place she called home, where so many memories, good and sad, resided?

She'd removed a thick pork chop from the freezer and put it in the refrigerator that morning, but it wasn't completely defrosted. She could zap it in the microwave to finish the job, of course, but she really wasn't hungry, and was even less enthusiastic about the prospect of cooking, though all she had to do was pop it in the oven.

She thought about the chicken wrap she'd half eaten at the hospital, but that immediately led her to recollect the man she'd sat across from.

She was being silly. Perhaps it was Richard's illness, seeing him in the hospital bed, that was making her sentimen-

tal, recalling her mother's long, slow decline. Yet her mind
wasn't conjuring up images of her mother or Richard. It was
focused on the thirtysomething man who'd sat across from
her drinking coffee and eating apple pie.

CHAPTER THREE

JIM LATIMER DIDN'T LEAVE the hospital until after dark. His uncle had stirred several more times, grown restless, made indistinct sounds, but never actually regained consciousness or opened his eyes. Still, the doctor hadn't given up hope that he would come around. His vital signs were strong.

Jim left his cell phone number at the nurses' station in addition to making sure it was noted on the patient's chart. Then he drove north to Mooresville on Lake Norman to pick up his son, Billy, at a friend's house. He and Eddie Farrell were in the same class in school. Billy had been slow to make friends since his mother died, and being in a strange place for the past month only complicated matters, but the two boys had been paired up to do a project together in class, and that had been enough for them to form a bond. Jim had met Eddie's parents, so when Leslie Farrell offered to pick up Billy from school and let him stay at their house until Jim could pick him up in the evening, Jim jumped at the chance and was very grateful for it.

"Is Uncle Rich going to be all right?" Billy asked, as soon as his father appeared. Jim knew the boy was scared. Richard was seventy-three years old, not a young man, but that was of no significance to an eleven-year-old. All he knew was that someone else he loved might die, just like his mother.

"We hope so. He was restless this afternoon. The doctor says that's good, that he's getting ready to wake up."

They gathered Billy's school books and coat, then Jim thanked Leslie, who dismissed the kindness as nothing special, while Billy said goodbye to Eddie. Jim and his son walked to the car in somber silence.

"Is he going to die?" Billy asked, once they were underway.

"I don't know. I hope not, but he is very sick."

"Like mom?"

"This is a different kind of illness. If Uncle Rich does wake up, he may not be able to do the things he used to."

"Like walk and talk. You told me. But he'll still know who I am, right?"

"I hope so, but we can't even be sure of that. It depends on how much damage has been done to his brain and what parts of it have been affected by the stroke."

"I don't want him to die."

Jim reached over, rested his hand on his son's shoulder and gave it a comforting squeeze. "I don't want him to die, either. All we can do now is pray, wait and see."

Later that night, after seeing Billy to bed and wishing him a good night, Jim returned downstairs to the den. His uncle's house, a mansion really, was huge, far too big for a solitary bachelor, which was one reason Jim had accepted Richard's invitation to stay there until he figured out what he was going to do. Now, with Richard in critical condition, the future was even more uncertain.

He was tempted to pour himself a drink at the wet bar, but he knew liquor wouldn't help, and he didn't want even a hint of it on his breath if his son called out to him. He remembered it too well on his own father's breath and the feeling of helplessness that came with it. You couldn't reason with a drunk. Sometimes you couldn't even predict what a drunk was going to do. Jim was determined his son would never have to face that particular uncertainty or the fear that accompanied it.

Jim had always been close to his uncle, closer than to his own father, who, even in the best of times, seemed to have a problem playing by the rules. Jim knew that Richard, as the older brother, blamed himself for that, though he shouldn't. Walter Latimer had made his own decisions, his own choices.

Around midnight, Jim finally went to bed, only to toss and turn with worry about his uncle and his son. And about himself. He'd always enjoyed a challenge, whether it was athletic competition, scholastic achievement or doing things on his own terms. The prospect of taking over PDQ Racing, however, was daunting. He'd kept the books for million-dollar accounts, but that wasn't the same as managing a high-profile multimillion-dollar enterprise.

As he gradually settled into that vague place between wakefulness and sleep, images of Anita Wolcott focused and faded. Her fiery red hair, the intensity of concern in her emerald-green eyes. Lisa had been gone almost two years now. A long time for a man to be without the companionship and comfort of a woman. Oh, he'd looked, even calculated at times. He was, after all, a healthy male in his prime, but beyond the physical attraction, he'd felt nothing. Lisa had been his world. Lisa and Billy had composed his universe. Now it was just Billy.

Until today. Okay, one brief contact in a hospital room,

a quick exchange of information in a cafeteria, was hardly the stuff of romance, but it *was* enough to stir coals.

Anita was undeniably attractive, but there was something about the way she carried herself that added to her appeal. Something more than her stylishness, more than her sophistication. Something in those green eyes that betrayed sadness—or loneliness, perhaps. Of course, they had been in a hospital. He supposed that could explain it.

He remembered holding her shoulders when she turned away from his uncle's bed and nearly tripped over him, and the momentary look of fear that morphed into confusion and finally defiance. She didn't pull out of his grasp, but held her ground and made him retreat. He liked that. It showed willpower and emotional toughness—and a challenge.

It was a few minutes past nine the following morning, as Anita was getting ready to leave her house, when her cell phone rang. She checked the caller ID and was surprised— and maybe just a little excited—to see Jim Latimer's name.

"Good morning," she said brightly after pressing the button to make the connection.

"We need to talk."

Uh-oh. "Is everything all right? Richard hasn't—"

"My uncle's condition hasn't changed. Where can we meet?"

He was obviously angry about something. She was tempted to say she would go to wherever he was, but that would amount to meeting on his turf, to putting him at an advantage.

"Where are you?" she asked.

"At the hospital."

"Do you know where the Coffee Can is on North Tryon?"

she asked. It was about midpoint between her house and the hospital.

"I'll find it."

"I'll meet you there in twenty minutes."

He disconnected.

What could possibly have him so steamed up?

She got there in fifteen, was lucky enough to find an empty booth in the back, sat so she could monitor the door and ordered a latte and a crumb bun.

He was five minutes late when she saw him come through the door. He must have had his radar working, because he zeroed in on her almost immediately. She waved and he strode toward her.

"Sorry I'm late." He dropped onto the bench seat across from her. His yellow-knit, collared polo clung to his shoulders and upper arms just tightly enough to emphasize their mass. "Back home we have a coffee shop called the Coffee Cup. Their sign is blue, so I guess that, without realizing it, I was looking for a blue sign here."

She'd observed it before. People, especially men it seemed, not being able to see what was right in front of them because it didn't look exactly like what they expected.

"It's brown," she said, "the color of roasted coffee."

The waitress came over, pad and pencil in hand. Jim asked for French roast, black. He glanced down at the bun Anita had barely touched and said, "I'll have one of those, too."

Was this a kind of olive branch after his abrupt manner on the phone? More likely he just liked crumb buns.

"Do you need a refill?" he asked, motioning toward her half-empty cup.

"I'm fine." Which wasn't altogether true. She found the man distracting and that didn't please her. Her life had finally settled into a pattern she was enjoying. She didn't need any distractions.

They should have made small talk while they were waiting for his order to be delivered, but since neither of them seemed to know what to say, they said nothing. He appeared to be as uncomfortable as she felt as he glanced around at the coffee house that had a slightly '60s hippy feel to it, an era that was before her time.

The waitress brought his coffee and pastry, along with a small jug of warm milk.

He started to tell her he hadn't ordered milk, but she was already walking away. One sip of his coffee produced a grimace followed by an ironic smile. He added the steaming milk.

"You issued a press release this morning," he stated, "disclosing my uncle's medical condition."

Ah, so that was it. "Yes, I—"

"And last night you contacted Bart Branch and his crew chief, Philip Whalen. They called me this morning."

"Yes." She was about to elaborate, but he again cut her off.

"Let's get something straight, Ms. Wolcott. Until my uncle wakes and demonstrates his competence, I'm the team owner, the person in charge. I run PDQ Racing. In the future, if MMG wants to continue to represent this team, you will confer with me before you notify the press on any matter, and you will not communicate information to team members behind my back."

Her heart pounded, as insult and fury battled inside her.

Yesterday, Sandra had given her carte blanche to issue the very press release he was now complaining about. As for the comment about communicating information behind his back, she regarded it as a direct assault on her integrity and professionalism, both of which she took great pride in.

Her impulse was to tell him to go to hell, to hit back as hard or harder than he had just assaulted her. But her sense of self-preservation, and maybe just the slightest twinge of guilt that she hadn't coordinated with him before releasing the notice, gave her pause. It wouldn't have been hard to do. She had his personal telephone number, after all.

"We're not getting off to a very good start, are we, Mr. Latimer?" she said, refusing to break eye contact with him. "For the record, I told you yesterday afternoon that we would have to issue another press release very soon in order to control the rumor mill. I gave you adequate opportunity at that time to object or to at least raise questions about it. You did neither. I took that as assent, as I would have with your uncle. You're correct. We need to establish some ground rules. In the meantime, I apologize for stepping on your toes. I didn't mean to."

When he stiffened at the jab to his pride, she knew she should have stifled the last comment.

"As for talking behind your back—" she took a deep breath "—Bart and Phil left messages on my cell yesterday afternoon. I returned their calls and told them exactly what you had told me. No more. I might also point out that they called me because they didn't know about you. They were able to phone you only because I gave them your number. I grant you, you didn't authorize me to pass it on, but then you didn't tell me not to, either. I saw no reason—you certainly hadn't given me one—to believe any harm would be done by keeping *your* team informed of Richard's health and the unlikelihood of his immediate return."

She started to take a sip of her coffee, realized her hand was shaking and released the handle without lifting the cup off its saucer. She could feel tears trying to squeeze out, but she wouldn't let them. One thing she was determined not to do was cry.

Another second slipped by. Then he blinked.

"I'm sorry, too," he said contritely. "I was out of line." He expanded his chest and huffed. "This is all very new to me." He let out a nervous laugh. "I guess that's pretty obvious." He raised his coffee cup and held it between them. "Truce?"

He'd actually apologized. That was something. Now if she could just get her heart to stop pounding. She hooked her finger into the handle of her cup again and was pleased when she was able to lift it without splashing coffee all over the table.

"Truce," she said, touched her cup to his and tried to smile.

They both sipped, settled, and let a minute go by in silence.

"My uncle was very pleased with the job you and MMG have been doing for the team. I don't want to change that. All I ask is that you keep me informed about what you're doing and be patient with me if I keep asking questions."

"Ask all you want," she replied. "We're both on the same side."

CHAPTER FOUR

ON FRIDAY MORNING, after seeing his son off on the school bus, Jim was once again reviewing his uncle's financial records. The situation was serious, if not grim. Cash flow had been negative for over a year—and not in small amounts. Richard had poured several million dollars of his personal fortune into the PDQ coffers. Even now, with a new sponsor on board for Bart Branch, the stock-car racing team was barely breaking even.

Jim was studying the list of recommendations he'd developed for his uncle—a list he'd never had an opportunity to present—when the hospital called to say Richard had finally regained consciousness and was asking for him.

On the half-hour drive from Lake Norman to the medical center, Jim's mind conjured up wishful images of the dapper gentleman lounging in his bed, laughing at his nephew's needless concern. He maneuvered his dark green SUV into a parking space near the hospital's main entrance. After hurriedly conferring with the doctor on duty, he stood on the left side of his uncle's bed. The older man had an iron grip on his wrist, like a drowning swimmer, afraid to let go.

"Take…over," he said with painful slowness, his speech badly slurred.

What the physician had described as some residual paralysis was far more serious than Jim had anticipated. The entire right side of Richard's body was virtually paralyzed, his right arm and leg useless. That side of his face also sagged; its muscle control was non-existent. Remarkably—blessedly—his mind seemed to be clear and unaffected, his thought processes normal and rational, though his ability to communicate was severely impaired.

It broke Jim's heart to see his uncle in this condition—this man who was able to bounce into a room and light it with his cheerful presence—struggling now for words, emitting sounds that were embarrassingly unintelligible. Jim wondered if he was supposed to actively guess the things Richard was fighting to enunciate, finish phrases and sentences for him, essentially putting in his mouth the words he couldn't get out himself, or let him labor through each torturous syllable. Doing so seemed cruel.

The doctor and physical therapist, ever the optimists, expressed confidence that, with determination and hard work, their patient's condition would improve. But that was the operative word. *Improve.* They couldn't say how much, though they made it clear he would probably never again be able to function the way he used to. That this alive, jovial, generous person, this intelligent friend, was reduced to grunts and spastic movements was so unfair.

"They'll have you up and about in no time," Jim protested, wishing with all his heart it were true, hoping by some miracle it might be.

"S-stup-pid," the old man roared in a three-syllable stammer, the last one explosive.

Whether he meant the comment was stupid, don't take

me for stupid, or don't you be stupid, wasn't exactly clear, but the underlying message was. He knew he would never be the same.

"T-time…you—" an exhausted pause followed for a few seconds, then "—t-team."

Jim mulled his dilemma. He was equipped to be a fiscal advisor; but, as much as he enjoyed watching stock car races, he didn't know anything about managing a NASCAR team.

"Lawyer," Richard mumbled.

"I'll call him."

"Anita…"

For a second, Jim's pulse spiked. Irritation or intrigue? Probably a little of both. There would be time enough for publicity and press releases later. But he wasn't about to argue with the sick man. Besides, the prospect of seeing the gorgeous redhead again had a definite allure.

"Hel-p y-you."

Richard expected him to seek help from a public relations rep? Perhaps the fox in the henhouse analogy wasn't entirely apt, but it came close. What PDQ needed now was sound management, not the illusions created by spin.

"I'll get in touch with her, as well," Jim promised.

Later that day, the senior partner of Kullberg, Castle and Slater arrived at the hospital with two assistants toting attaché cases crammed with legal documents and forms. Jim met them in the lobby, and the four of them went together to Richard's room. Anita was already at his bedside, chatting with him about rankings and point spreads, as if nothing had happened. After a few minutes of solicitousness, Leland Kullberg embarked on a series of questions that required only assent or denial on the part of his client. When he was finished, he an-

nounced that Richard Latimer, while physically impaired, was
of sound mind and that he had requested that his nephew,
James Latimer, assume ownership of PDQ Racing.

Papers were signed and witnessed. Seals were affixed.

"I'VE PREPARED A PRESS release," Anita said, after they left
Richard's room and the lawyers had departed.

"Already?" Jim asked, automatically accepting the piece
of paper she removed from her portfolio. "The ink isn't
even dry on the transfer documents yet."

"I'm doing my job, Jim. There's no reason to keep this
under wraps. A release now puts us in front of the rumor
mill, rather than in reactionary mode, responding to other
people's questions."

She watched his dark eyes as he digested what she said.
His nod acknowledged, grudgingly, that she was right.

"Okay," he said, rattling the single sheet of paper in his
hand. "Let me read this."

The press release was straightforward and to the point.
It announced in a very businesslike fashion that, due to
health problems, Richard Latimer had decided to hand over
operational control of PDQ Racing to his nephew, James
Latimer. It summarized some of the achievements of the racing team since Richard had established it, sang the praises
of their current driver, Bart Branch, and his crew chief,
Philip Whalen, and promised that its pursuit of excellence
in the NASCAR Sprint Cup Series would continue under his
nephew's leadership. It also expressed thanks for the thousands of good wishes Richard had received from friends,
colleagues and fans for his speedy recovery.

"May I make a couple of suggestions?" Jim asked.

She got the impression of playfulness in the question, but she couldn't be sure. She was having trouble reading this man. Polite and abrupt. Accusatory and apologetic. Serious, yet with a sense of humor.

"Of course," she said casually, stifling the impulse to remind him that since he was the boss, he could make any damn change he pleased.

"Refer to me as Jim rather than James, and say my uncle has decided to hand over *temporary* control of PDQ to me."

She felt a bit of the pressure inside her subside, accepted the paper back from him and said, "Easy fixes. I'll get this off right away. I have a question, though."

He gazed at her, waiting. "Yes?"

"This weekend is the race at Dover. Are you planning to attend? Either way, you'll have to let your uncle's motor-home driver know today."

"It's impossible," Jim said. "Uncle Richard has been awake less than twenty-four hours. His chances of having another stroke are still very high, from what I've been told, and my leaving him now might very well exacerbate matters."

"I understand and completely agree," she said. "So I have a suggestion."

He crooked an eyebrow, again waiting for her to continue.

"You haven't had a chance yet to meet with the team, and it's traditional for the owner to give them a sort of pep talk before a race. How about I set up a video-teleconference? You can introduce yourself to them from here, either Saturday evening or Sunday morning, whichever works best for you. It won't be as good as your personal presence, but it'll show them you're involved."

He smiled. "Good idea. I never thought of that."

She tried not to feel smug. "That's why you have me, Jim. I'll get this off—" she shook the press release in her hand "—then make the arrangements."

She started toward the elevator.

"Anita," he called out.

She turned. "Think of something else?"

"Do you have plans for dinner this evening?"

For a moment she stopped breathing. The image that came instantly to mind was of an intimately dark restaurant with starched white linen, a single candle flickering in a crystal flue. Wine sparkling in the rationed light.

Then sanity kicked in, and she remembered they still had a lot of details to go over and a public-relations program to work out. Discussing business over a meal wasn't exactly a novel approach. People had to eat and time was limited. Richard Latimer had been a relatively laid-back manager, who delegated low-level decisions to subordinates and rarely questioned them once the wheels were set in motion. Judging from Jim's reaction to her talking to PDQ's driver and crew chief, she thought it unlikely he was inclined to be nearly as passive.

"What time would you like to get together?" she asked. "And where?"

"I still have a few things to take care of first. Can I call you? I promise it'll be within an hour."

"That's fine. You have my number."

He cracked a smile. "Stored in my memory bank."

INVITING HER TO DINNER HAD been an impulsive thing to do. Jim didn't think of himself as an impulsive man, but he had to do something to make up for his boorish behavior yesterday morning. Maybe an unhurried meal in a pleasant restaurant would ease some of the tension that had sprung up between them.

He couldn't shake the image of her sitting across from him in the coffee shop, telling him—oh, so calmly, politely and reasonably—that he was a damn fool. That wasn't the part that bothered him, though. He'd been called a fool before, and a few times he'd even deserved it. No, it was the hurt look in her eyes when she stared over at him, refusing to be cowed, refusing to back down. She'd been at the point of tears, shaking like a leaf in rage and injured pride, yet she'd valiantly refused to give an inch. Quite a woman.

A fascinating woman. And a beautiful one.

Maybe dinner would give them a chance to get off to a new start. Maybe, too, he'd get to know her better. This wasn't a date exactly. He'd been away from the dating scene a long time, and in truth, he wasn't sure he knew how to play the game anymore. The world had been a lot different when he was courting Lisa. Or at least *their* world had been. Now he was in the world of NASCAR. Were the people here so much different?

Perhaps tonight he'd find out.

CHAPTER FIVE

THE NAME THAT APPEARED on Jim's caller ID late Friday afternoon was a surprise.

"Jim, this is Gideon Taney." The owner of Taney Motorsports, Will Branch's team. "I just wanted to call and tell you how sorry I am to hear about Richard. I hope things turn out all right. I also saw the press release announcing that you've taken over PDQ, and I wanted to welcome you to the brotherhood of racing-team owners."

Was this a formal organization? Jim had never heard of it, but then he was so very new to all of this. "Thanks, I think."

Taney laughed. "A bit overwhelming, if you aren't prepared for it. Actually, it can be overwhelming, even when you think you are."

"It's nice to know I'm not just a slow learner."

Taney chuckled softly. "Look, I won't keep you. I imagine you're up to your elbows in alligators right now. Your uncle and I have always gotten along well. I have the highest respect for Richard, and so I thought I'd pass on to you that I'm available if you ever feel the need to talk, owner to owner. Discreetly," he added.

"Thanks, Mr. Taney. I appreciate that."

"Call me Taney. Everybody does."

"I go by Jim."

"Well, Jim, you'll find you can't sneeze in the garage area without half a dozen people handing you a tissue, but some of us are capable of keeping a confidence. I don't believe in letting the press in on things before their time, if you know what I mean. So if you start thinking of selling, or just want to knock ideas around, be sure to give me a call."

"Sell," Jim repeated, not as a question as much as a rein-forcement of an idea. "I haven't even considered it."

"Maybe not yet, but at some point you will. When that time comes, I hope you'll put me at the top of the list of people to contact. In the meantime, good luck with the team, and please pass my best wishes on to Richard."

After hanging up the phone Jim leaned back in the big swivel leather chair behind his uncle's desk.

Sell.

Add that to the list of options. If Richard recovered suffi-ciently to take over again, the idea would be moot. Jim had no doubt his uncle wouldn't easily give up his "obsession." But if he didn't get better… If Jim was forced to take over full control and found himself inadequate to do the job, or it demanded time that he needed to devote to Billy, selling might be the best solution. So, along with hiring a general manager, Jim would have to consider selling the team altogether.

How well would Bart get along with his twin brother if they were on the same team? They were competitors *now*. Could they also support each other as teammates? Will had a reputation for being a bit of a hothead under pressure, but he was a good driver.

All of this was idle speculation, of course. In the end, if

Jim did decide to divest himself of the team, Taney Motorsports would logically go to the top of the list of potential buyers. The deciding factor in the sale, of course, would be the bottom line. Who would pay the most?

Perhaps, Jim reflected, he ought to work up some figures in order to be prepared if the subject ever became an active point of discussion.

As he jotted down a note to himself, outlining what data to gather for such an estimate, he had to ask himself how his uncle would feel about it. Richard had spent two decades building his team and its reputation. It had become the center of his life. The idea of selling smacked of betrayal, and Jim felt sure that was how Richard would see it, too. Still, a good manager hoped for the best and prepared for the worst.

One thing was certain. He wouldn't tell anyone about this. Not his uncle. Not Bart Branch or Phil Whalen. Definitely not Anita Wolcott.

OVER THE NEXT FEW HOURS Anita reviewed the myriad of things she and Jim needed to discuss. There was the busy publicity program she was developing to promote Bart Branch as a driver, rather than the son of a man who may have pulled off one of the biggest bank heists in history. And she wanted to present her ideas for a campaign to entice EZ-Plus Software into renewing their sponsorship for next year and hopefully more seasons after that. A long-term relationship between a sponsor and team was to the advantage of both, since it established what was called a brand in the minds of fans, the instant association of one with the other.

She was proud of her work. She liked her job, enjoyed meeting people, interacting with them, getting her message across. She had to wonder, though, if her new boss would appreciate her efforts and could respect her for her thoroughness and professionalism, even though he didn't think much of the profession itself.

The restaurant Jim had selected for them to meet gave her pause. Why Chez Wolski? It was hardly the setting for a hard-hitting business conference, more the type of place you invited a guest to in order to impress them. Why would Jim Latimer want to impress her, especially when he seemed to have such disdain for her occupation? Of course, business could be discussed just about anywhere. Still, Chez Wolski seemed an unlikely choice. Or maybe, like his uncle, Jim simply enjoyed good food and good service.

She arrived a few minutes early. If this was strictly business, she didn't want to keep him waiting. If he had something more "friendly" in mind…well, she wasn't into playing games.

She rose from the built-in wooden bench on the left side of the waiting area when he entered the restaurant. Again, she was struck by his physical presence. Maybe not movie-star handsome, but definitely head-turning, with a stance and a presence that exuded male strength and confidence.

"Thanks for coming," he said, checking his watch. "I hope you haven't been waiting long."

"Only a few minutes. It's one of my flaws, being chronically early."

"Hmm." He grinned. "That's good to know. So if you're ever late, I'll know you're actually standing me up."

"No, no, no," she objected, "I'm not about to abdicate my prerogative as a woman to be late."

The hostess came out from behind her podium, large folding menus in hand. "Ready?"

Anita had never been to this restaurant, and she quickly realized it had an uncanny resemblance to the daydream she'd had when he'd initially proposed they get together for dinner. The hostess led them through a maze of small rooms and cozy alcoves, while the tantalizing scents of butter, garlic and spices assailing them in waves.

"I hope I'm not interfering with plans you had for this evening," he said, as they were seated in a quiet booth by a window. *Like a date.*

"Well, there *were* some TV commercials I wanted to watch."

He laughed. "Maybe you can catch the reruns."

They were presented with the menus, then the young hostess lit the candle in the glass globe on the table and left.

"In your job, you probably eat out a lot," he said, after the hostess left them.

"An occupational hazard."

"I should have thought of some place more original for us to get together then."

She realized her response may have come across as a put-down, which wasn't how she'd intended it at all. Not a good start to the evening, whether they were there professionally or socially.

"Actually, what I meant was—"

He gave her a humor-filled smile. "No offense taken, Anita. I like honest answers." He chuckled. "I'm so used to fast-food places, I don't even recognize the names of the things listed here." He made a show of perusing the menu, his thick, dark brows drawn together in bewilderment. "Where are the quarter-pounders? I had no idea this place was…well, like this when I made the reservations. Lucky choice."

She wondered.

The waitress arrived and asked what they wanted to drink. Both opted for a glass of white wine.

"There's—" Anita began.

"I need—" Jim said at the same time.

She grinned. "We seem to keep bumping into each other, if not physically, verbally." *I think I like the physical collisions better,* she mused.

"You first," he said.

The wine arrived, and the waitress took their dinner orders.

"My boss received a call this morning," Anita told him, "from Mark Jessup at EZ-Plus. He's the vice president for promotions. I don't know how familiar you are with the sponsorship side of the business—"

"EZ-Plus Software took over sponsorship of Bart Branch's car after his father disappeared."

Anita nodded. "Mark wanted to know the status of Richard's health and the team."

"What did Sandra tell him?"

"That Richard is awake and alert but may be turning the team over to you temporarily."

"With your press release out, he knows that's a done deal now."

Again Anita couldn't decide if Jim was just stating a fact or expressing a negative judgment.

"I'll call him first thing in the morning," he said. "I wish we'd had more time to coordinate the details of this transfer. I don't like people thinking they're being ignored. But Uncle Richard was very insistent that it had to be done right away."

"I'm sure it gives him peace of mind to know his affairs are in good hands." At Jim's frown of doubt, she added,

"He's strong, Jim. He'll pull through." She took a sip of her wine. "How long have you been involved with PDQ?" She'd met all the employees, and he hadn't been one of them. She would certainly have remembered.

"Uncle Richard called me about six weeks ago. Said his chief accountant, Otis Mulroney, wanted to retire and asked me to audit PDQ's books. He also casually mentioned that, since I was the only one in the family who'd ever shown any interest in his obsession—that's what he calls it—that I might as well get to know the business from the inside out since someday I'd probably inherit the team. I figured that wouldn't be until years from now."

"Were you planning to take over as chief accountant when Mulroney retired?"

"That's what my uncle wanted me to do, and I was giving it serious consideration. I've been an independent CPA since graduate school and have really enjoyed it, but it's very time consuming, especially at tax time. That wasn't really a problem when Lisa…when my wife was alive. We learned to adjust to it. But as a single parent, I need a nine-to-five job, which is what Richard offered me."

For a moment, Anita felt battered, then foolish. It would have been natural to assume he was married. Most thirty-something people were. Why hadn't she considered that Jim Latimer might be? Because he wasn't wearing a wedding band? A lot of men didn't. More disturbing was that he was a widower. How had his wife died? In an accident? Illness? Then came the shocker that he was a parent, as well. How many children did he have? Boys or girls? And what were their ages?

"I'm sorry to hear about your wife," she said. "May I ask how long ago she passed away?"

"It's been almost two years now."

"I am sorry," she repeated, then added, "Those words always sound so inadequate. How many children do you have?"

"Just one. A son. Billy just turned eleven."

"It must be difficult for both of you. I should warn you, if you don't already know it, that being an owner definitely won't be a nine-to-five job, unless you plan on hiring an executive vice president or chief operating officer to manage the day-to-day details of the company in your stead."

"That's an option, but it's not what I really want to do," he admitted, "or what Uncle Richard would want, which leaves me with a dilemma." Tension tightened the corners of his mouth. "My number-one responsibility is my son. As much as I love my uncle, Richard comes second, and PDQ, frankly, ranks third." With a weak frown, he added, "Probably not what you wanted to hear."

She took a sip of her wine. "I don't advise telling the team that. For NASCAR professionals, especially those at the heart of the action, NASCAR is number one in their lives. Everything else is a distant second. It's a matter of priorities. I certainly understand and respect yours. Family comes first, especially where children are involved. As for your uncle, I don't think he'll pose much of a distraction from your responsibilities to the team, so I guess the real question is how much distance there is between your responsibility to your son and the NASCAR team you now own."

CHAPTER SIX

"IF ALL GOES WELL," JIM said, enjoying the way the candle-light danced in her red hair, like tiny golden sparkles, "I'll only be in caretaker status for a short while until Uncle Richard recovers. If he doesn't, though, or if he doesn't recover sufficiently to take over again, I'll have several tough decisions to make."

"Where's your son now?" she asked.

"Staying with a schoolmate tonight, his first night away from me since we moved here."

Jim had left his cell phone number with the Farrells. He hoped they wouldn't have to call him, but he couldn't rule out the possibility.

The food arrived. Anita admired the presentation, commented on how good it smelled and picked up her fork. He found himself more interested in observing her and admiring the grace of her movements than in the food.

"I thoroughly enjoy NASCAR," he said a minute later, after they'd sampled their first bites. "Billy and I love watching the races on TV and seeing them in person when we're able to get to a track. But I'm certainly no expert in the sport, not like my uncle. Nor am I the businessman he is."

"You can learn," she offered, sounding positive and upbeat. It was amazing how much her vote of confidence lifted his spirits. He'd almost forgotten how much he missed a woman's encouragement.

"The question is—how fast and whether I can keep my hours sufficiently under control to be there for my son when he needs me. He's lost his mother, Anita. He's upset now because his Uncle Rich, with whom he's become very close, is seriously ill. I don't want him to feel he's lost me, as well."

"Of course you don't."

They ate in silence for a couple of minutes. The food was expertly prepared, beautifully displayed and presented in quantities that satisfied without being overwhelming.

"How about you?" he asked. "Any kids?"

She grinned across the table at him. "Shouldn't you ask me if I'm married first?"

He snickered, even as he shifted uncomfortably in his seat. "Okay. Are you married?"

"No."

"Didn't think so. No wedding ring or sign of one, and you don't strike me as the type of woman who would accept a dinner invitation with a man, married, single or otherwise, if there was a husband or significant other in the wings."

"You seem to have me all figured out."

"I meant that as a compliment," he said, intrigued by her reaction.

She acknowledged it by lifting her wine glass and toasting him with it. When their eyes met, hers sparkled with amusement. "And to answer your first question, no kids."

By choice, he wondered, or had she just not found the right man? Did she want a family or was her career the driving force in her life? Then he had to ask himself soberly why he cared. That he did, was disconcerting and exciting at the same time. He hadn't come here with the intention of flirting, and this minor exchange hardly qualified, but the fact that he was enjoying himself, enjoying being with this very attractive woman, added an extra shot of adrenaline—or perhaps testosterone—to his system.

"How long were you married?" she asked a minute later.

"The first time or the second?" He laughed at her startled expression. "I like to think the first time doesn't count. It was a childish adventure on both our parts. Janie and I were still in college, full of ourselves, convinced we had the world by the tail, not to mention being swamped in a sea of hormonal urges." Like he seemed to be right now. "It took almost a year for us to discover—or maybe I should say admit—we were basically incompatible, sex aside. We split the sheets, went on to graduation and haven't seen each other since."

ANITA BROKE OFF A PIECE of bread, entranced by the sound of his voice. Deep, mellow, his drawl mild, lulling. Even his marital misadventure was more than she'd experienced. She'd dated occasionally in high school, but had never gone steady. In college, she'd dated even less, not that there hadn't been offers, but by then, her mother's condition had deteriorated to such an extent that social services were providing caregivers so Anita could attend a limited number of classes during the day. She had to pay people to stay with her mother in the evenings, so dates had become a luxury that were at best time-limited.

She envied him—or rather the women who'd shared his bed.

"Lisa and I met the following summer," he went on after a sip of wine. "We were married three months later."

"Love at first sight." Yes, she could imagine that with this man. Under different circumstances, of course. For all the crystal and white linen, the candlelight and fine service, this was a business dinner, and she had to remind herself of that.

"Billy was born a year later." Jim smiled sadly. "He was nine when Lisa died. Ovarian cancer. How'd you get in the P.R. racket?"

The quick change in subjects was a jolt, but she understood why. She tried not to take offense at the implication in his choice of words.

"I began working for Sandra Jacobs part-time when I was still in college. Mostly administrative stuff, but it gave me an opportunity to learn, and before long, I discovered I liked what I was learning."

"When did you go full-time?"

"Two years ago, after my mother passed away."

"It's my turn to say I'm sorry. What about your dad?"

"Died when I was ten. How about you? Where are you from?"

"Tennessee, near the Kentucky border. My folks have a horse farm up there."

"Race horses?" Her interest was piqued. She'd always wanted to ride—for pleasure, not competitively—but she'd never had either the time or money.

"Not the kind you're probably thinking of," he said. "No Thoroughbreds in our stables, no Kentucky Derby contenders. We raise standardbreds for harness racing."

"A horse-racing background," she mused and tried to picture him atop a mighty steed, but not in a jockey's racing silks. The image of him that came to mind was in muscle-hugging riding breeches and the red coat of a country gen-tleman, a crop in his hand, hounds at his feet. "And now you're into NASCAR. A natural progression, I suppose."

He laughed—that warm, sun-filled sound that she was beginning to really like. "Not really. You can't love a stock car the way you can a horse. I grew up with horses, love the sight of them, even the smell of them."

She was enthralled by the animation on his face, the sparkle in his eyes. She had no doubt he was telling the absolute truth from his perspective. She wanted to tell him that NASCAR devotees experienced the same kind of rapture about their cars, that for them, even the numbers had an aura, just like they did for him as an accountant. But she doubted he'd believe her. Until he experienced it for himself, he couldn't possibly appreciate the spell. Besides, she was having much too much fun soaking in his earnestness to interrupt him.

"I thought for a long time that I wanted to be a horseman," he went on, "until reality reared its head. I'm a decent rider, but for all my exposure to harness racing, both trotters and pacers, I have no talent as a driver."

"It's that difficult?"

He chuckled, and this time his humor made her uneasy. She'd obviously said something stupid.

He softened his tone. "Do NASCAR drivers actually have special talents?"

"Touché." She took another sip of her wine.

"We all have things we're good at, and if we're really good at doing them, we make them look easy. I'm good at crunching numbers, which I imagine most people think is about as stimulating as watching paint dry. But I enjoy it and

I'm good at it. Your job is a lot more exciting than mine, a lot more challenging, too."

He'd just complimented her again, she realized, but it was a hook with a barb. *You stay out of my business and I'll stay out of yours.* Fair enough.

"You still have family back in Tennessee?" she asked.

"My folks and my in-laws. Their place is right next to ours."

"Moving here must have upset them."

"It did, and I don't mind telling you I seriously hesitated. As you can imagine, my wife's death hit my son pretty hard. I've had a few problems with Billy getting into fights, giving his grandparents a bad time. When I brought up our possible move to his therapist, however, she thought the change of environment might be good for him, a kind of new start. So I left the decision up to Billy. To everyone's surprise, mine included, he said he wanted to come here."

"How's it working out so far?"

He rocked his head gently from side to side. "It's really too early to tell. At the moment, everything here is a new adventure."

"And now his great-uncle is in the hospital. You said you've been here a month. Why weren't you at the race Sunday?"

He nodded acknowledgment of the seeming indifference. "I'd planned for us to be there, but then my aunt called to remind me Sunday was my mother's birthday, as well as my parents' anniversary, and since Billy and I weren't home, she thought it would be a good idea for us to come back and spend the day with them. After all, there would be plenty of other races for us to go to."

He shrugged his broad shoulders and tilted his head slightly to one side. "I couldn't dispute the logic, and Uncle Richard was all right with it."

Anita appreciated his dedication to his family, and she envied his having a large, apparently close-knit, one. Her own parents had been only children, so her network of relatives was extremely small. Still, she sensed friction in Jim's family. She had no idea what the source might be, but his willingness to move away from them suggested some sort of tension.

It was none of her business. If he chose to tell her about it, and she hoped he did, she would certainly listen, but she wouldn't impose on his privacy by asking.

"You said your uncle asked you in to audit the books," she commented. "Any particular reason, other than the chief accountant's retiring?"

"My specialty is fiscal analysis. PDQ has encountered a couple of rough years. Caley Mitchum's bailing out as Bart's sponsor in the middle of the Nationwide season two years ago, then losing BMT as a sponsor this year, has put a significant strain on resources."

"Richard was able to get EZ-Plus for the balance of this season—"

"But at a much-reduced rate," he pointed out. "In the meantime, he's been pouring his own funds into the team."

"I didn't realize money was getting tight. His reputation as a philanthropist—"

"My uncle is an extraordinarily generous man. He's given millions to charity over the years, as well as supported various members of the family. But in the last few years, he hasn't been paying as much attention to his personal investments as he should, and his income has been dwindling."

"So he wanted you to help him figure out where to adjust."

"No question, he has to stop the bleeding."

"And your recommendations?"

He broke off a piece of bread and spread butter on the edge. "Mostly administrative and technical changes, none of them particularly painful or controversial. The big one…well, there's no question the weak link and our biggest liability right now is our driver."

"You're not suggesting replacing Bart Branch?"

Jim shrugged. "So far, he hasn't shown himself to be NASCAR Sprint Cup Series caliber—"

"He won in Charlotte," she pointed out, an edge intruding into her tone.

"Thanks to the Lucky Dog rule."

Whenever there was a caution flag, the Lucky Dog rule allowed the leading car in the one-lap down pack to move up to the back of the lead pack when the caution was lifted, essentially giving the driver a free lap.

"So what?" she objected. "He won the race, fair and square. He played by the rules. Other people moved up, too, thanks to the Lucky Dog rule. Are you going to disqualify all of them?"

He snorted. "I'm not disqualifying anyone, Anita. My point is—"

"What exactly?" she demanded.

His eyes momentarily widened at her sharp challenge. He blew out a breath. "He has only finished in the top ten three times this season—Bristol, Martinsville and Texas."

"Don't forget his win last weekend."

"Fluke. Twenty-three drivers have not made the top ten at all this season."

She almost laughed. He may not be a NASCAR fanatic, but he obviously knew the rules and kept up with statistics. *Accountants!* she almost snapped. "You think they all deserve to be fired?"

His brows narrowed. "Please don't twist and distort my words, Anita. You're not in front of a microphone. You don't have to demonstrate your prowess as a spin doctor."

She stared at him. Her insides tightened. No question of his disdain for her profession now. Her heartbeat chugged in her chest, and a feeling of helplessness swamped her in the face of his undisguised contempt. Well, this wasn't about her, she reminded herself, but about the team and loyalty to the people who formed it.

"There's also the matter of his family problems," Jim went on. "They keep getting worse. Maybe after they're resolved, Bart will be able to concentrate on racing and do better, but right now they're distracting him from doing his best. Also, sponsors, except EZ-Plus Software, aren't interested in being associated with people involved in massive fraud."

"You're being unfair and judgmental," she said, pushing her plate back from the edge of the table. "He's not responsible for what his father's done—assuming, of course, his father *is* the guilty party. For all we know Hilton Branch could be dead and buried somewhere or a hostage, a victim himself."

Jim picked up his wine glass. "I'm just saying—"

"Kick the guy while he's down."

"Whoa—" He lowered the glass without drinking and peered at her. "Anita—"

"Do you have any idea what Bart and the other members

of the Branch family have been through since Hilton disappeared?" she asked, undeterred. "Virtually all their assets have been frozen, including their personal accounts. If it weren't for what Will and Bart have earned as drivers *since* their father's disappearance—"

"Anita, please calm down. I'm not suggesting Bart is involved in his father's shenanigans. I understand better than you realize that he's not responsible for his father's actions and that he doesn't deserve to be tarred with the same brush. I'm certainly not suggesting he be fired on the spot."

"You wouldn't save any money by firing him now anyway. He has a contract." She glared angrily at him.

"All I'm saying is that, if he doesn't make the cut for the Chase, that we start looking for another driver for next year, because with all his family baggage, without a positive season he's going to have a hard time keeping EZ-Plus as a sponsor or getting a new one."

"There are dozens of drivers who go on from year to year who don't make the cut."

"I want PDQ to be a team of winners, not just also-rans."

A lofty goal, one she shared, but she wasn't placated by his ideals. Not that Jim Latimer had any obligation to appease her. She was, she reminded herself, as her blood continued to run hot and fast, a subordinate, an employee, the hired help.

"Are you going to tell him this?" she asked. "Or will you wait until the end of the season and then drop it on him that he need not bother coming back next year?"

Jim arched a brow and shook his head, clearly disappointed by her attitude.

She knew she was making him sound like some heartless villain, entrapping and manipulating unsuspecting victims into impossible situations. But everyone knew the name of the game was winning. For all his problems and flaws, Bart did, too.

"I haven't made any decision yet." Jim took a deep breath, then added, "Last week I was an accountant. Now I'm a team owner. You asked what I was going to recommend to my uncle, and I told you. Replacing Bart Branch, and…that would have been up to Uncle Richard to decide."

"And now, you have to make the decision," she concluded.

"Now, I'll have to make the decision."

CHAPTER SEVEN

A TELEVISION CREW BIG enough to do a full documentary showed up Sunday morning at Richard's house. Jim and Anita had discussed where and when to stage Jim's video conference with the team. He'd been in favor of the PDQ headquarters in Charlotte. But most of the team would be gone, she argued, and an empty garage area wouldn't be very inspirational. She'd favored the hospital, perhaps with Richard in the background, but that raised problems with the hospital staff, who felt it would be disruptive and would cause their patient too much stress.

They finally compromised on using Richard's large, dark-paneled den, which was filled with awards he'd received over the years, plus dozens of framed photographs of him with NASCAR officials, drivers, crew chiefs, movie stars, politicians and other celebrities. Anita said it was important that Jim be seen as carrying on his uncle's traditions, and this setting was a good, tacit acknowledgment of that. Jim positioned himself at his uncle's desk.

He and Bart Branch had spoken twice on the phone since Jim had taken over. The conversations, neither of which lasted more than a few minutes, had been friendly but stiff, as if the two men were sizing each other up.

Over those same three days, Jim had spoken three times to Phil Whalen, Bart's crew chief. To say the two men were comfortable with each other would have been an exaggeration, but they were definitely more at ease than Jim and Bart.

"We have a connection," the technician announced.

Phil's face appeared on the large plasma screen across from the desk.

"Hi, Jim. Good to see you," Phil said, as if they were old friends. "We're all here."

The camera swept the other end of the room. Jim could see rows of people, most of them in team uniforms.

"Hello, everyone. For those of you who don't know me, I'm Jim Latimer, Richard's nephew. I met some of you last year at the races in Bristol and Indianapolis, and I hope to meet the rest of you in person in the not-too-distant future. I'm happy to report that, while Richard is experiencing some paralysis on his right side, he's doing well. You can be sure he's receiving the finest medical care available. He sends his regards and asked me to thank all of you for the many flowers and cards you've sent.

"Now you're about to face the competition at Dover without him being there to cheer you on and lend his moral support. He tells me this is the first NASCAR race he's missed since he established PDQ nearly twenty years ago, so you know he'd be there with you, if he possibly could.

"I'm not going to bother with the usual pep talk about doing your best. You certainly don't need me to inspire you to do your jobs. You're all extremely lucky people to be able to do something you obviously love so much."

He paused for a moment.

"Many years ago, before any of us were born, there was a radio sportscaster in the Midwest who later went to Hollywood and became a movie star. One of his most famous roles was playing an inspirational athletic figure. There was a line from that movie that became famous and followed him all the way to the White House. I'm going to unabashedly use it now and apply it to my uncle. Perhaps you can keep it in mind today when you're rolling out the No. 475 car." He paused again, then smiled. "Let's get out there and win one for the Gipper."

BILLY RAN INTO THE HOSPITAL room Sunday afternoon and bounded up to the bed, a broad smile on his face. "Hi, Uncle Rich. I brought the latest copy of the *Race Car Ledger.* It's just come out. I thought you'd like to see it."

The seventy-three-year-old grinned crookedly. "Good." Then he mumbled something Jim didn't understand.

"That's all right," Billy replied, apparently having no trouble deciphering his words. "I'll read it to you while we're waiting for the race to start."

Jim smiled, momentarily overwhelmed with poignant melancholy. It had been his idea to have Billy read to his mother in her last month. Children's books then, but it didn't matter. Those moments bound them together forever and brought them both joy. Now Billy was prepared to do it again, this time for his great-uncle. Jim was proud of him.

Richard came out with another stream of gibberish.

"What did he say?" Jim asked.

"That it's hard for him to read sometimes, because he can't always focus his eyes real good."

"Oh."

Richard grinned and mumbled some more.

Billy unconsciously puffed out his chest.

"What?" Jim asked again.

"He says it's a good thing one of us can understand him."

It was true that Billy seemed to have little difficulty figuring out what Richard was saying, better than anyone else, in fact. For Jim it was like listening to a muffled telephone conversation. He could decipher occasional words and phrases, but he was unable to make much sense of them.

Using his left hand, Richard upped the volume on the TV. The race at Dover was about to begin.

Twenty minutes later, a nurse came into the room and tried to turn the set off, claiming it was upsetting the patient. Richard's reaction was a loud rage that got Billy upset.

Jim ushered her out into the hallway.

"My uncle is the owner of PDQ Racing. He has a car in today's race. You're going to cause him to blow a gasket if you turn off that TV or change the channel."

"Oh, I didn't know that. Still…"

"It's the one pleasure he has left, watching the team he's built over two decades. Don't take that away from him."

He could see she didn't like being opposed, but she relented.

Over the course of the four-hour race she and several other staff members came to the room for updates on what was happening. Bart Branch gained several fans that afternoon, and Richard took on celebrity status as a NASCAR owner.

Having qualified on Friday for fifth position, Bart started the race well, but he steadily lost ground, quickly dropping to eighth and never advancing above seventh after that. He ended up finishing eighteenth, earning him a hundred and nine points, but that still left him almost eight hundred points behind the leader. Bart's brother Will did even worse, coming in under the checkered flag in twenty-fifth place.

The winner that day was Dean Grosso, with his son Kent coming right behind him in second place. Kent, a fourth-generation NASCAR driver, was doing well this year; he was a force to be reckoned with, having taken second place at the season's opening race at Daytona, then winning the checkered flag at prestigious Talladega. There was a good deal of speculation going around that this would be his father's last season. At nearly fifty, Dean was the oldest driver in the NASCAR Sprint Cup Series. He had an impressive record of wins over the years, but he'd never won the NASCAR Sprint Cup Series championship.

"Don't…worry," Richard told Jim. "B-Bart w-will c-come through."

"I hope so," Jim replied, then added without thinking, "He'd better if he wants to race for PDQ next year."

"Time…grow!" Richard bellowed so loud Jim was afraid people would come running to find out what the commotion was all about. Richard's inability to control or perhaps to realize the volume of his speech was sometimes startling.

"I know," Jim said, not wanting to rile him further. "He still has plenty of time to turn this season around."

"Better."

Did he mean Bart had better improve? That he would do better? Or that Jim had said it better.

Jim missed the man he'd known all his life, who was always there with an encouraging word and a good story— Jim smiled to himself—and a good reprimand, if it was necessary to set things straight.

Throughout the race, as television coverage shifted to the pit and garage areas, Jim kept watching for glimpses of Anita. With her flaming red hair she wasn't difficult to spot, especially with her bright red-and-orange PDQ cap on.

There had been one very brief interview with her just before the race in which she touted Bart's driving qualities and expressed her certainty that he would do well, not just today but for the season. A prediction which, at least in the short term, turned out to be not quite accurate. But she was a spin doctor after all and did her job well for the good of the team.

"Be careful, you'll lose your credibility," Jim had muttered to the screen.

"Always positive," Richard responded, surprising him, since Jim didn't realize he'd said it loud enough to be overheard. Did he mean *always be positive* or *she was always positive?*

He glanced over at his uncle to find the good side of his face cracked in a cunning smile.

CHAPTER EIGHT

OVER THE NEXT COUPLE of days, Jim maintained a nonstop schedule. Being a CPA had never been this time-consuming or exhausting—or exciting. He followed up by phone and e-mail on the visits he'd previously made with sponsors. When the subject of Bart's poor showing came up, he took a page from Anita's playbook and minimized its significance by pointing out that it was only one race and that he had finished ahead of twenty-five other drivers. Maybe he was beginning to understand the art of spin, Jim decided, discovering guiltily that he was enjoying the challenge. He quoted statistics that showed that Bart was solidly in the running for both the Chase and the NASCAR Sprint Cup Series championship at the end of the season, and he did his best to reassure supporters that he knew how to manage a NASCAR team, that PDQ was in good hands. In the process, he almost convinced himself. Almost.

He'd been watching NASCAR races for years and consciously—or unconsciously—had accumulated a wealth of what he had thought up until now was essentially useless information, ranging from driver records and annual earnings to lap times and point spreads. He hadn't been lying to Anita when he said numbers were his forte. Maybe he didn't have a photographic memory, but in the realm of statistics, he came close. Intent on rounding out his education, he now found himself going to bed with racing magazines and journals, as well as articles and commentaries he'd copied off the Internet. He'd wake in the middle of the night in a pool of crinkly papers, like an undergraduate cramming for a final exam.

The primary-school year was due to end on Friday. Jim could simply have kept Billy out of class on Thursday and Friday so they could fly to Pocono and witness qualification and practice laps, but he wasn't big on breaking rules without an explanation. On Monday afternoon, he stopped by Billy's school and explained the situation to the principal.

"He has a good attendance record at his previous school and satisfactory grades," she pointed out, "releasing him early isn't a problem. What about his schooling next fall, if you're going to be tied up full-time with the team?"

Jim was hoping his uncle would be back in charge by then, but of course that was hardly a realistic approach. Hoping for the best was human nature, but a good manager planned for the worst.

"I haven't made any firm decisions yet," he replied. "A lot will depend on my uncle's level of recovery."

She nodded. "If I can be of any assistance, Mr. Latimer, please call me. I'll be glad to discuss various options with you."

On his way back to his car, he decided to call Anita. She might have some suggestions, and even if she didn't, he wanted to hear her voice. He hadn't seen her since their dinner at Chez Wolski, which had ended on a positive note after he'd assured her he wasn't committed to letting Bart go, that he was doing no more than trying to consider all the alternatives available.

A positive note, he repeated in his mind, but not one devoid of tension.

"How do NASCAR people handle schooling for their kids during the racing season?" he asked when she picked up.

"Some stay with relatives, grandparents, aunts and uncles or godparents so they can attend regular schools."

Jim could picture her relaxing at her desk as she held the phone to her ear. He imagined her red hair and her creamy soft complexion.

"A few send their kids to boarding schools," she added. "But the vast majority of them are homeschooled."

Just because PDQ was headquartered in Charlotte didn't mean Jim had to live there, especially if he delegated day-to-day management to someone else. He could return to Tennessee so Billy could be close to his grandparents. The only family Billy would have in Charlotte was his father and his uncle—if Richard recovered enough to come home rather than go to a nursing facility or into a retirement community. But that determination wouldn't be made for some time. Sending Billy to a boarding school was out of the question. To the boy, it would feel like abandonment, and to Jim, it would amount to betrayal of his role as a parent.

"Homeschooling makes the most sense," he said into the phone. "Except…I help Billy with his homework as much as I can, but I'm not qualified to do the actual teaching, and time management could still be a problem."

"I understand homeschooling programs come with detailed instructions on how to teach the individual lessons." She paused. "I can introduce you to several mothers who homeschool their kids, if you like."

"Thanks. Sounds like I'm going to need all the help I can get."

"Glad I can be of assistance." Was there sarcasm in her comment?

Jim arranged, again with her help, for his uncle's motor home to be driven to Pocono with instructions to Stu, the driver, to stock it with foods appropriate for Billy—his usual cereals and the kinds of healthy snacks Jim limited him to. He was beginning to appreciate how much he was coming to rely on Anita. As always, Richard's situation assessment was right on the mark.

"There's only the one bedroom," Stu pointed out, "with a king-size bed. But one of the sofas in the living area opens up into a queen. Probably not all that comfortable for an adult, but I doubt your son will even notice. Kids seem to tolerate thin, lumpy mattresses far better than us grown-ups."

"That's as good a plan as any for the time being," Jim agreed.

"You might want to look around for another motor home when you get a chance," he suggested, "one that's better-suited to your circumstances. Or have this one modified. They can change things pretty quick if you're willing to pay the price."

"Thanks. I'll check into it."

Jim knew, from his review of PDQ's financial status, that his uncle had paid over a million dollars for his motor home, one and a half million, to be exact. Jim's house back in Tennessee wasn't worth a quarter as much, and he was reasonably sure any significant modification to the motor home would run to at least six figures. Maybe millionaires could afford such extravagance—Jim didn't begrudge it to them— but he didn't consider himself a millionaire, only the steward of his uncle's estate.

He and Billy visited Richard on Thursday morning before they flew up to Pennsylvania on Richard's private jet. The doctors and therapist said not to tax the patient or get him emotionally excited, so Jim found himself holding back from asking his uncle questions he alone could answer.

"Wish I…"

Jim squeezed the old man's hand. "I wish you were coming, too," he said. "Be patient with yourself, do what the experts tell you, and you'll be up and around in no time."

Richard gave him a lopsided grin.

ANITA HAD JUST CONCLUDED a press interview on Thursday afternoon and was moving across the Pocono infield when she saw Jim walking purposefully toward the motor home lot, a boy by his side.

She waved her arms frantically to get his attention, since calling out would have been futile against the din of the crowd and the roar of engines in the background. Catching sight of her, Jim's face lit up, and she experienced a bubbling inside her at his welcoming expression.

As they drew closer, she studied the boy. This had to be Billy. Oh, my. The kid was going to be a lady killer in a few years. He looked remarkably like his dad. The same dark hair and olive-toned skin. Only the eyes were different. Instead of being coal-black like his dad's, the boy's were dark blue.

"Just get here?" she asked, unable to repress a smile.

"A few minutes ago." Jim placed his hand reassuringly on the boy's shoulder.

"You must be Billy," she said before Jim had a chance to make the formal introduction. "I'm Anita Wolcott. I work with your dad and the PDQ team to get the word out about how great NASCAR is, and them in particular."

He gave a shy nod.

"Have you been to a NASCAR race before?" she asked.

"Last year at Bristol 'cause it was close and I didn't have to miss school, and then in the summer at Indianapolis."

"Exciting races," she noted, "but that was before I was representing PDQ. That's why I didn't get to meet you. Does this mean you're ditching school today?"

"Dad got me out early. I have a reading list for summer, though."

She chuckled, hoping to put the boy at ease. "Seems like a fair compromise, don't you think? You would have gotten the reading list, anyway, right?"

"I guess."

"You like reading?"

He nodded. *"Harry Potter."*

She smiled. Who said kids wouldn't read books? Even long books?

Already, they could hear the howl of individual cars circling around them, their unmuffled, high-powered engines screaming into turns and exploding onto straightaways. Before long, that sound would be multiplied ten- and twenty-fold as more cars arrived and took to the track. On Sunday afternoon, forty-three cars would shake the ground and shatter the air with their combined roar.

"Tomorrow will be the qualification laps to determine the starting lineup."

"And see who gets the pole," Billy contributed.

"Exactly." The pole was the inside-front position. "Have you been to your motor home yet?" she asked Jim.

"We're on our way now."

"I'll go with you."

THEY WALKED DOWN THE LONG lane between rows of million-dollar palaces on wheels. It was probably just as well that Billy positioned himself between them, Jim decided, because otherwise he might have given in to the impulse to take Anita's hand in his in sight of the boy.

Along the way, she stopped three times to introduce him and his son to the owners who had their motor homes parked nearby. One of them was Gideon Taney. He was three or four inches taller than Jim and broad-chested, with large hands and feet.

Remembering the phone call he'd received from Taney right after taking over PDQ, Jim was on guard about what the man might say now. The place was buzzing with media types, and even if none were around at the moment, there was always someone willing to feed the rumor mill with sightings and real or imagined overheard remarks. The slightest hint that he and Taney might be involved in any sort of discussion would probably start a speculative frenzy about what they were up to. That wasn't necessarily bad from a P.R. perspective. Drumming up public interest in a team was what gave sponsors exposure and sold products. Anita had also pointed out that it was better to be proactive than reactive. At the moment, however, Jim didn't feel prepared to handle either approach.

Taney greeted Jim enthusiastically and with a vigorous shake of the hand, but he did so as if they were total strangers who had never spoken to each. He inquired into Richard's health and smiled approvingly at the news that the old timer was making progress.

"Sorry, but I've got to run," Taney said, backing off. "Another meeting to attend. You know what it's like." With that he disappeared at a trot.

They hadn't progressed another ten yards when Anita stopped again. This time she introduced Hugo Murphy, Justin Murphy's uncle and crew chief.

"How's Richard doing?" Hugo asked. He had a lantern jaw, dark hair and sharp, penetrating eyes.

Jim repeated the current report. They, too, shook hands, and then Hugo headed toward the garage area.

"Everybody knows Uncle Rich," Billy said.

Anita nodded. "And everybody likes him."

At last they arrived at a motor home sporting a pennant with the PDQ red and orange team colors.

Jim poked numbers in on the keypad beside the door. Inside was a distinctively masculine world. Nothing in the rich decor hinted at a woman's influence. No floral designs. No feminine knickknacks. The color scheme was predominantly brown and black; a rust-accented stripe in the overstuffed upholstery was the only splash of color. There was cool chrome where a woman would have chosen warm copper or bronze, dark wood where she might have preferred lighter tones.

Jim flipped a switch and the indirect lighting imparted a remarkably cozy glow. Perfect for relaxing with a snifter of good cognac after a busy day. Hardly a setting that was appealing to an eleven-year-old boy, however.

Without asking for permission, Anita went to the picture windows on both sides of the living area and opened the slatted blinds to let more sunlight spill in. "That's a little better, don't you think?"

"It *is* a bit of a morgue in here, isn't it?" Jim remarked.

Billy went over to the sofa opposite the wide-screen TV, grabbed the remote off the coffee table and turned it on to race coverage. The narrator was discussing the lineup for the day and the expectations for the various drivers. Apparently not interested in what was going on right outside the motor home, the boy accessed a video game with the dexterity of a computer geek.

"I don't want you spending all your time playing video games," Jim announced sternly.

His son looked at him with the kind of long-suffering impatience that Jim suspected the teenage years would perfect.

"What do you want me to do?" he asked, just shy of impertinence.

"Do you play soccer?" Anita asked Billy before Jim could respond.

"Sure. I'm on the team at school."

"Good. Let's see if we can find Ryan Palmer."

"Who's he?"

"His mother is Will Branch's rep, like I'm Bart's." She flipped open her cell phone and poked a couple of buttons. "Hi, Kylie. Where are you? Is Ryan with you?" After a brief exchange, she snapped the instrument closed. "They're in Will's motor home. It's not far."

Jim looked at his watch. "Okay, but then I need to head over to the garage area, talk to the team, go up to the hospitality suite and check with the caterers about the spread for

Sunday, after which I've also got a couple of dozen phone calls to make."

"The busy life of a race-team owner," Anita quipped.

Jim's smile sheltered a frown. "Uncle Richard always made it look effortless."

"Who was it said professionalism was making the difficult look easy?"

He laughed. "A sage, I'm sure."

Back outside, they walked a little farther down the line to their right. The roar of high-performance engines on the track had already increased in volume.

"I know Bart and Will Branch are twins," Billy commented. "I've seen their pictures, and they look exactly alike. Is it true, even in person, people can't tell them apart?"

"Some people can't," a male voice came up beside them. "But I can. Hi, Anita."

She looked over and smiled. "Hello, Carl." They all stopped. "Carl Edwards, I'd like you to meet Jim Latimer, Richard's nephew. He's taking over PDQ."

CHAPTER NINE

"TEMPORARILY," JIM emphasized and extended his hand. "This is my son, Billy."

"Wow. Carl Edwards. Car No. 99." Jim smiled at his son's wide-eyed expression. He, too, shook the famous driver's outstretched hand. "Hi, Mr. Edwards," the boy said breathlessly.

"Pleased to meet you, Billy. Where are you all off to?" he asked Anita.

"Thought I'd take him down to Will's to meet Kylie and her son. Billy plays soccer in school. I figured the two of them would enjoy kicking the ball around."

"Cool," Carl said, smiling at the youngster. "If I can get by the soccer field later, maybe you'll let me bounce a few off you guys."

"Awesome."

"How's your uncle doing?" Carl asked Jim.

Jim repeated the latest progress report.

"Be sure to give him my best." He turned to Billy. "Have you ever met Will or Bart?"

"I met Bart at Bristol last year when I went there with my dad and at Indianapolis."

"Are you sure it was Bart?" Carl asked him, his eyebrows

raised skeptically. "They like to trick people by impersonating each other, you know? Have you ever known twins? Go to school with any?"

"Bobby and Ronny Schmidt, but they don't look anything alike. Some people don't even believe they are really twins."

"That means they're fraternal, not identical, like the Branch twins. It's true most people can't tell them apart, but I can."

"You can?" Billy gazed up at him with wonder.

"Yep. There is one sure way to distinguish them. Know what it is?"

The boy shook his head, intrigued.

Carl leaned down and whispered in his ear. The boy's face lit up, and his deep blue eyes twinkled in merriment at being let in on the *secret*.

"Hey, I've got to run," Carl announced, straightening up, "or my crew chief will think I'm playing hooky. See you later." He and Jim shook hands again. "Enjoy the race," he called out to Billy, as he ran toward the garages.

"What did he tell you?" Anita asked.

Billy shook his head and grinned smugly. "I'm not going to tell. That's between Mr. Edwards and me."

They arrived at a motor home that was very much like the others around it; only a few minor details distinguished it from its neighbors. Anita mounted the steps and tapped on the door. Within seconds, a slender woman with neatly trimmed brown hair opened it. Jim had met Kylie Palmer, Will Branch's P.R. rep, at MMG, a few days after he'd taken over as owner of PDQ Racing.

"Hello, Jim," she said and immediately focused on his

son. "You must be Billy. Come on inside." She swung the door wide so they could enter.

Sitting on the couch in the living area past the kitchen was Will Branch, wearing his gold-and-black uniform. He put down the papers he had been reading, got up and came over to greet his guests.

"Mr. Latimer, I'm pleased to meet you." They shook hands. "Sure was sorry to hear about your uncle. How is he doing?"

Jim felt like an answering machine as he once more repeated the condensed version of Richard's condition, but he was also gratified by the genuine interest so many people showed in asking the question. Richard really was liked and respected.

He introduced Billy. Jim could sense his son evaluating whether this was really Will or his brother pretending to be him. He grinned to himself.

Not far behind him stood a boy a little shorter than Billy. Kylie introduced her ten-year-old son, Ryan.

"Billy plays soccer," Anita explained. "So I thought maybe the two of you—"

"All right!" Ryan shouted and raised his hand for a high five. "I brought my ball. Want to go kick it around?"

"Can I, Dad?" Billy asked anxiously.

Jim hesitated. Billy was generally independent in familiar surroundings, but this was foreign territory.

"They'll be fine," Kylie assured him, obviously reading his thoughts. "There's a ball field over by the campgrounds. Everybody knows Ryan, and he has a cell phone if he needs anything, or if you need to get hold of Billy."

"Sure," Jim replied to his son.

Ryan had already retrieved his black-and-white soccer ball from the corner near the door.

"We met Carl Edwards on our way here," Billy told Ryan. "He said he might come by later and play with us."

"If he does," Will told Ryan, "give me a call. I can kick a ball better than he can any day. I'll give him a lesson."

Ryan's face lit up. "You got it, dude."

"Ryan," his mother intoned critically.

"Sorry. Mr. Branch."

Will smiled and shrugged. "Just let me know."

In a flash the two boys were gone. A minute later, Jim excused himself and left, as well.

KYLIE MOTIONED TO ANITA to stand by for a minute, then extracted a piece of paper from the zippered leather satchel she'd deposited on the granite counter separating the kitchen from the living area. "I'll leave this schedule with you, Will. Check it over and let me know, as soon as you can, if there are any problems. I know the appearances in Nashville and Knoxville are tight, but I think they're doable. Same with Atlanta and Greenville. If push comes to shove, we can do the Greenville interview by telephone, but a personal appearance will be better."

He shook his head, but with a smile on his face. "No rest for the wicked."

"I think the expression is no rest for the weary," Anita corrected him.

He chuckled. "My brother is weary. Wicked is much more fun."

"I'll let him know." She laughed. "On the other hand, maybe I won't."

Outside, the two women walked toward the track press office.

"So how are you and Jim getting along?" Kylie asked.

"Fine so far." *But then we haven't had time to talk yet today.*

Kylie laughed. "He sure is hot."

Hot! Her word for him, too. It still amazed her that they were talking about an accountant.

"Definitely a good-looking guy," she allowed casually.

Kylie cast her a skeptical grin. "Honey, if you think he's only good-looking, you haven't got your eyes fully open. How'd your dinner go?"

"You know about that?"

"Where'd he take you?"

"Chez Wolski."

"Mmm, nice. Did he kiss you goodnight?"

Anita stopped and stared at her friend. "Of course not. It wasn't that kind of—" she almost said *date* "—occasion."

Kylie snickered. "Sometimes I wonder about you, Anita. So sheltered." She put her hand lightly on Anita's arm and leaned toward her. "Honey, when a man takes a woman to Chez Wolski for dinner, it's always that kind of occasion."

Was she right? Jim had said he didn't know what kind of restaurant it was when he'd made the reservations. She'd been on dates to less fancy places. Had he been coming on to her and she was too naive to realize it? If so, their discussion had destroyed any atmosphere he might have been trying to establish. She shook her head, and they resumed their walk to the press room.

"You've got it all wrong," she insisted. "It was nothing like that."

"Let's see," Kylie went on, as if her companion hadn't

spoken. "After asking you how long you'd worked at MMG he elicited your life story, then he told you his."

Anita scrunched up her mouth in irritation. "What else would two strangers talk about? Don't make something out of this it isn't, Kylie. We could and probably would have had the same conversation at a pizza joint."

Kylie's eyes twinkled merrily. "That's right. But you didn't. He took you to Chez Wolski instead."

Anita shrugged, annoyed with the obvious truth of the statement. "Sounds like you have an answer for everything. But I repeat. There was no goodnight kiss." *Darn it.*

PHIL WHALEN ARRANGED FOR Jim to meet each member of the team as they arrived at the Pocono garage area, then to address them all at the start of their group meeting in the hauler lounge at six o'clock that afternoon.

At the appointed hour, Phil called the noisy assembly to order, the murmurs gradually died down, and he introduced Jim.

The place was packed, so Jim had to squeeze up to the spot Phil had just occupied. He turned and let his eyes roam over the faces before him.

"You've all got an advantage on me," he said, after reintroducing himself. "You only have to remember one new name. I've got a roomful to memorize."

He allowed a moment for everyone to get relaxed, himself included.

"I know you all are worried," he said, "about what will happen to the team while my uncle is laid up. So is he. That's why he asked me to take over PDQ. It's something I'm honored and proud to do, but I'm the first to tell you it's also intimidating and I do it with some misgivings. I don't have his charm and personality, and I certainly don't have his years of experience. That's where you all come in."

He looked out over the sea of faces. On each of them he saw interest, but some were more leery than others. Fair enough, he thought.

"In the course of the weeks and perhaps months ahead, I'll be coming around, looking over your shoulders, asking what you're doing." He smiled. "Some of my questions will probably sound pretty darn stupid, too."

A chuckle of polite amusement rippled through the audience.

"The reason I'm telling you all this is because I don't want any of you to think I'm challenging you or the decisions you make in the course of doing your jobs. I'm simply trying to learn. So please be patient with me. I'm an accountant, after all, a bean counter, for heaven sake—"

The laughter was more relaxed and sincere this time.

"That's why I need each of you to help educate me."

He saw a couple of nods of agreement, even approval, but most remained stoically polite and probably not convinced.

"I'm the new kid on the block."

And they all made it clear from their expressions that it would be up to him to prove himself to them, not the other way around.

CHAPTER TEN

ANITA CALLED JIM ON HIS cell phone and established his whereabouts—in the PDQ hospitality suite high atop the grandstands.

"I'll just be a few more minutes," he said.

"We have half an hour yet before your press conference, but I thought it would be a good idea to go over things one more time before you enter the lion's den."

"You do my morale wonders," he jested. "Why don't you come up here? We can talk things over on our way back to the press room."

The PDQ suite was the same size as its neighbors, but each was uniquely decorated according to the owner's taste. In this case Anita entered what looked like a nineteenth-century frontier barroom. A period-piece mahogany bar stretched across the back of the inside wall. Half a dozen old-fashioned round oak tables, surrounded by spindly armchairs were informally arranged deeper into the middle of the room, a Tiffany lamp hanging over each.

If it resembled the set from *Gunsmoke,* that was because it was. Richard had purchased the pieces in an auction shortly after he'd acquired the suite. The bartender on Sunday would sport a handlebar mustache as well as sleeve garters and a white apron around his middle.

Along the far side wall was a buffet, bare now, but on race day, it would be crowded with a variety of foods on silver platters and in steaming chaffing dishes. Jim was standing near it with a tall, slender woman who held a clipboard.

"Peeled shrimp," she said, running her finger down a list. "And a round of beef with the usual rolls and condiments. Tamales, chicken flautas and beef tacos. Did you decide on the crab cakes?"

"Them, too," Jim said. "Drummies, chicken tenders with honey-mustard sauce, and the customary chips and dips."

There would be sixty-eight people here for the race, including Jim, his son and Anita. Invited guests would include sponsors, potential sponsors and corporate executives, politicians and dignitaries, as well as their spouses and families.

Anita wandered over to the counter at the top of the balcony, and sat on one of the stools facing the massive window that constituted the entire outside wall. The room offered a commanding view of most of the track, especially the finish line. The plush theater-style seats, set in descending rows, were far more roomy and comfortable than the un-upholstered seats in the stands outside.

Getting to observe a NASCAR race from this vantage point was prestigious and posh, but, Anita thought wryly, this wasn't the place to *experience* a race. The room was air-conditioned and soundproofed. You didn't get to hear the roar of the engines or feel the ground shake as packs of cars streaked by at a hundred and eighty miles per hour. And from high up here, in this sterile environment, you couldn't smell the hot asphalt, the pungency of lubricants and raw fuel or the acrid stench of burning rubber.

"Sorry to keep you waiting," Jim said as he approached.

He was wearing a well-tailored business suit, white shirt and blue-striped tie. Conservative. Nothing loud like Richard was wont to wear. Staid. Sensible. Everything in order. That was Jim. It also occurred to her that he fit this room. Whether he realized it or not, he fit right in.

"I just spent more money on food and drink than I earned last year," he said, when he came over to join her. "And this is only one race."

"You'll get used to it."

He laughed. "That's what I'm afraid of."

"You ready to go?"

"Yeah," he said, offering her his arm.

THE IDEA OF STANDING BEHIND a bunch of microphones and answering questions off the cuff wasn't something Jim had ever done before, and it was definitely not a prospect he relished.

Kylie caught up with them on the way over to the press booth. "I hear you did a great job in your teleconference last weekend," she observed.

He started to ask her who'd told her that, but it had to be Anita. Who else would? He was tempted to get annoyed. Hadn't he made it clear to her that he didn't want her discussing team business with other people? But Kylie wasn't exactly an outsider. She was, but…

Anita might not have told her directly. Maybe she'd told Sandra, her boss, and Sandra had passed the word on to Kylie. Since they worked for the twins and the report was positive… Jim realized he was trying to justify Anita's action, yet a week ago, his response had been just the opposite.

"As for this news conference—" Kylie tilted her head to-

ward Anita "—you've got one of the most thorough coaches
in the world. You'll do fine."

"I certainly hope so," he murmured, agreeing with her
about Anita but still not feeling nearly as confident as the
two women seemed to be.

They proceeded to the press center. An interview with another team owner was just ending. Everybody was laughing.
Apparently the other guy was an old pro at this sort of thing,
which made Jim all the more self-conscious about his own
inexperience. He stepped onto the platform as the other guy
was stepping down.

Anita situated herself in front of him and stood confi-
dently at the podium. Without any hemming or hawing, she
identified herself for the benefit of the camera and explained
that the founding owner of PDQ Racing, Richard Latimer,
had recently suffered a stroke and had passed on management of the team to his nephew, Jim Latimer. She then introduced Jim.

There was no applause, hardly a murmur. This was a press
conference, after all, not a pep rally or an awards ceremony,
and the anticipatory silence between Anita's words and his
getting into position at the mic was intimidating.

He gave the short opening statement Anita had helped
him craft and which he'd memorized. To his ears, it sounded
exactly like what it was, rehearsed and artificial. What surprised him was that, as he looked out at the sea of faces, no
one appeared to notice or care. Fighting the urge to bolt, he
then said he'd be glad to answer questions.

Secretly he was in dread. He'd been on the debate team
in college, but that had been a decade and a half ago. He'd
studied up on NASCAR and memorized the additional in-

formation Anita had given him, but anything could happen where the press was concerned. There was always the surprise question he wasn't prepared for. In that event, Anita advised him to say he didn't know the answer, if that was the case, rather than make one up and regret it later, but it was the "have you stopped beating your wife" type of question he dreaded the most.

"How much experience have you had in managing a NASCAR team?" a reporter in the front row asked. Jim had already explained in his opening statement that his background was in accounting and business consulting, not in hands-on management. Hadn't the guy even bothered to listen?

"I've been following my uncle's team for years," he replied calmly, "though I've played no active role in its management till now." He was equivocating and expected someone to call him on it, but no one did.

"What kind of changes are you planning to make?" the man's neighbor asked, presuming change as a foregone conclusion.

"My uncle has built a fantastic team," he said, "one he can justifiably be proud of. I'm proud of it, too. The short answer to your question, therefore, is I have no plans to make any changes. This management adjustment is only temporary until my uncle resumes control." He wanted to glance back at Anita. To get her nod of approval? But she'd cautioned him against saying or doing anything that might suggest uncertainty or insecurity on his part.

"PDQ didn't exactly break any records last year," a woman in the back row pointed out. "And now with all the controversy surrounding the Branch family, Bart has good reason to be distracted, even if he isn't guilty himself of any wrongdoing. That doesn't bode well for the rest of the season."

Jim was momentarily jolted by the reporter's use of the word *distracted,* the same word he had used when discussing Bart with Anita, but more important was the woman's unfounded inference that Bart might be involved in his father's larceny. Jim was about to respond, to defend his driver's integrity and honesty, when he remembered something Anita had told him: don't answer questions that haven't been asked. The reporter was trying to goad him into a discussion of the scandal stirred up by Hilton Branch and more recently by Hilton's ex-mistress in her upcoming tell-all exposé.

"What's your question?" he asked instead.

For a moment the woman seemed flustered, either unaware she hadn't posed one or annoyed her provocation hadn't produced the result she'd hoped for. "Do you expect Branch to do better this year than he did last?" she asked peevishly.

"Yes." He sensed immediate dissatisfaction with the curt reply. Anita had recommended that he not alienate them. "Last season," he continued, "was a terrific learning experience. Bart and the entire team garnered a good deal from it. Last year we competed. This year we're going to be challengers."

"You sure haven't been so far," another reporter observed sarcastically. So much for journalistic neutrality. "At this point a year ago, you were in twenty-seventh place. Right now you're in twenty-ninth."

Jim waved the comment aside. "We're still three months from the Chase." Here, his statistical background served him well. He recited several specific cases over the past twenty years in which drivers had advanced from much worse positions to finish in the top ten, two of them actually winning the NASCAR Sprint Cup Series championship.

"This Sunday," he concluded, "you'll see us move up, and the Sunday after that we'll move up again."

"You think you still have a chance for the Cup then?"

"Of course we do. Nothing is guaranteed in this sport. We all know that. It's one of the things that makes NASCAR so exciting, but I have absolute confidence in the PDQ team to do its very best and that our efforts will produce results we can all be proud of." As he said the words, he realized he actually believed them, and he became aware of that confidence being projected into the platitudes.

Jim felt rather than saw a nod of approval from Anita, who had moved up to stand on his right as a sign that the interview was drawing to a close. There were a few more questions after that, all of which Jim handled with light humor and skillful dodging.

"You did great," Anita told him after they'd ceded the podium to the next team owner and were making their way to the exit.

"Nice of you to say so—"

"Anita is right," Kylie agreed. "You were an absolute natural up there."

"I was shaking in my boots the whole time."

The feelings that suddenly swelled within him—pride, satisfaction at seeing Anita's approval of his performance—surprised him. It had become as important as Richard's opinion. What he also knew was that the real challenge still lay ahead.

CHAPTER ELEVEN

"NINETEENTH PLACE," PHIL Whalen told Jim the following afternoon when the starting positions were finally posted after the qualifying laps.

"In the forward half of a field of forty-three cars," Jim muttered. "Could be worse."

While Billy played with his new friend, Jim attended the team strategy meeting in the hauler. In addition to Bart, Phil, the head of the pit crew and the spotter, there were the engineers who would help configure the car for the peculiar conditions of this track.

How a driver handled a car when he was in the first quarter of the lead pack and how he drove when he was at the end of the second pack were quite different. Frontrunners had to hold their positions, which meant spending a good deal of time eyeing the rearview mirror. A mid-pack driver had a much harder job because he had to protect himself front and back, be on the offensive as well as the defensive and use his brakes more often.

In any case, having a good spotter at the top of the grandstands, giving continuous reports of who was where and how they were positioning themselves, was crucial. Driver visibility was extremely limited. Without outside eyes keeping him apprised of what obstacles lay ahead and what chal-

lengers were closing in from behind, a driver was left im-
possibly vulnerable.

"We've got a different setup here," Phil Whalen said,
standing in front of a visual projection of the race track. "It's
a long track, two-point-five miles, but it's not your usual oval
or D-shape. This one is triangular. An isosceles triangle for
those of you young enough to remember your high-school
geometry. Three different length sides, which means three
different angles. The toughest one isn't the sharpest but the
narrowest."

He pointed to the curve at the top of the diagram. "Turn
Two, known as the tunnel turn is shallow-banked, only eight
degrees, and the groove will allow only one car to go
through at a time. Try to stay abreast of the other guy in the
turn and you'll end up against the wall, so your fight is going
to be for the approach. Of the straightaways, the front
stretch is the longest."

Jim watched Bart as he took this all in. He still didn't feel
he knew his driver. The guy had been running hot and cold,
aggressive and passive. He needed more wins, or at least a
couple more top-five finishes to restore the kind of confidence that fed on itself and bred passion in fans and
sponsors. Maybe this race would be the one. Jim hoped so.

He listened to the team members discuss a wide range of
topics. He was way out of his element when it came to the
technical details of stock car racing. These guys were the
experts. Based on Bart's experience in both the practice and
qualifying runs, they debated tire pressures and the use of
suspension wedges, but alterations might still have to be
made again during the race itself. The situation was always
fluid, forever changing. And of course, there was the critical

subject of pit stops. Fewer was always better, but running out of gas wasn't an option. The number of tire changes would also affect pit times and the car's handling on the track.

At the end of the meeting, Phil asked Jim if he had anything he wanted to add.

"You've all practiced and know your jobs," Jim told them with a modest shrug. "I've watched and timed and studied your performances in comparison with other teams out there. I understand now why my uncle has always been so proud of you individually and as a team. You all have what it takes. On Sunday I'm convinced you'll prove it."

His sentiments were echoed across the room, and the traditional cheering and palm slapping ensued before the group split for the night. Still, Jim made his way outside with niggling doubts. By now, he had met all of the team members, learned a little about their personalities, their families and backgrounds. He sincerely believed what he said, that they were all pros at what they did and were dedicated to victory, but there was something missing from the equation, some indefinable quality.

Alluding to these reservations as he and Anita walked back to his motor home, he asked her if she knew what it might be.

"Your uncle. You miss him and so does everybody else. He's always been at the heart of the team. I've seen him rally it with the sheer force of his personality."

"A talent I don't possess."

She cast him a sympathetic glance. "I think you're projecting your own insecurities into the situation. Have faith in your team and they'll come through, but first you have to have faith in yourself."

No one had ever accused Jim Latimer of being faint of heart. He'd excelled at school, been the captain of his college soccer team, and when the family crisis had come along, he'd been the one who had rallied everyone and gotten them through the shame and humiliation. Of course, he'd had Richard supporting him the entire time, morally and financially. The situation was drastically different now. In a sense he'd become his uncle, the man wielding the power.

Anita's quizzical expression told him she expected some sort of a reply, but what she didn't know wouldn't hurt her.

ON SUNDAY AFTERNOON when the 500-mile race finally got underway, Jim was atop the war wagon, headset in place, listening to the chatter between his team members. It had taken him a while on Friday and Saturday to get his "ears," the ability to decipher the muffled sounds coming through his headphones, to distinguish one voice from another and to crack the code of jargon that zealots of every endeavor reserved to themselves. It was frustrating at times but compellingly fascinating, too, a world unto itself that throbbed with constant excitement.

"Four-eighty-six high," Jim heard the spotter report. Car No. 486 was Jem Nordstrom's. Bart was just pulling out of Turn One. He stomped on the gas going onto the straightaway toward the bottleneck of Turn Two.

Bart pulled in tight against the inside as he accelerated.

Nordstrom was alongside Bart. Now it was a game of chicken to see who would take the "tunnel" turn first.

"Hold tight," Jim whispered, though he had his mic turned off and no one around him could possibly have heard him above the roar of the cars flashing by.

Nordstrom crowded Bart from the right but apparently didn't have the power to pull ahead of him.

"Hold your ground, dammit," Jim urged. "Make him back off."

But as they approached the turn, Bart lost his nerve, let off on the gas and Nordstrom shot ahead of him into Turn Two.

Jim let out a stream of profanity—at least in his mind. In the roar vibrating through him, he couldn't be sure if he'd actually vocalized the words.

No guts, no glory. Dammit!

Two more times, Bart let himself be maneuvered out of the lead going into that same tight turn, and twice more Jim felt his temper rise and his morale plummet. Anita was wrong, he decided. He wasn't projecting his insecurity. It was being reinforced by his driver.

"Oh, no," Jim muttered on Bart's 287th lap. "Don't..." Not that it made any difference. He had the earpiece snugly in place but no microphone, and even those standing within inches of him couldn't possibly hear him over the wall of sound bombarding them from the track. He could see what was coming and knew it wouldn't be pretty.

"Back off," he heard Phil tell Bart. "You're too close. Back off."

Jim's attention swept from the action around him to the small TV screen atop the wagon. It was clear there, too, that Hale Garrett, driving car No. 418 was trying to shake Bart off his tail, but had no room to maneuver. With cars on either side of him, he couldn't weave to break the draft coming from behind him, which left him only one option, slow down. But that wasn't easy, either, not with a car sitting mere inches from his tail, sharing his airspace. Besides, there wasn't a driver alive who wanted to slow down, not on a straightaway. A more experienced NASCAR Sprint Cup Series driver wouldn't have put himself in this spot, but Garrett was a rookie out to prove himself.

Jim knew, even as he witnessed it, that there would be a lot of debate about what happened next. Did Bart intentionally move forward and tap car No. 418, or did car No. 418 slow down and thereby cause the bump? Whichever it was, the result was the same. Bart's front bumper came in contact with Garrett's back bumper just as they were going into Turn One, and the laws of physics took over.

Garrett's tail drifted right. The change in attitude slowed his forward momentum, but the interruption of the stream of air slipping over Bart's car slowed him, as well. The car on Garrett's inside left moved forward unmolested, the car on his right did the same, but only because he was able to maintain the higher speed. The same good fortune didn't apply, however, to the car immediately behind him. In less than a heartbeat, Garrett spun into the path of No. 426, which was advancing on his right. Bart then hit Garrett and was himself rammed by No. 437, which had been directly behind him. The three cars were all pulled to the right by the centrifugal force of the turn. Car No. 426 hit the wall, bounced back, and before anyone could sort it out, a chain reaction had six cars spinning helplessly down the back-stretch.

Bart hit the grass verge of the infield sideways. The sudden impedance on his left side caused him to roll and kept him rolling, side over side over side. Four spectacular tumbles until he came at last to rest upside down.

The yellow caution flag sliced frantically through the air.

Everything settled into slow motion. The pace car came out and led the pack around the track, as damaged cars were driven, pushed and pulled off the race way by crew members and emergency vehicles.

Bart's car must have blown its radiator. Steam was vaporizing from under the hood. All eyes were on him when a minute later he crawled out of the driver's-side window, stood up and waved victoriously to the crowd.

"So much for catching up on points in this race," Jim muttered and hoped nobody had heard him.

"What do you think of your driver's performance today?" a lone reporter asked Jim later as he was making his way from pit road through the garage area.

Anita miraculously appeared at Jim's side.

"He ran a good race today," she declared before Jim had a chance to speak up. "He was moving up steadily until—"

"He crashed and took five cars with him," the reporter reminded her.

Anita made light of it—or tried to. "This is NASCAR. Stuff happens. It's what makes every race different and exciting. No one can ever predict what's going to happen next."

They moved on another few paces. "If Bart can maintain the momentum he was building in this race," she continued more seriously, "he'll be in the lead going into the Chase, and he'll be snatching up his first NASCAR Sprint Cup."

"Absolutely," Jim piped in, buoyed by the sight of her brilliant red hair and energetic pace. "I won't use the hare and tortoise analogy. They're all hares in this sport, but consistency and steady progress have a lot to be said for them."

He and the reporter spoke for another few seconds. Satisfied with his sound bite, the newshound ran off to get another sage opinion.

"Thanks for saving my bacon," Jim told Anita after the guy was out of earshot.

"Judging from the sour expression on your face, I figured I'd better."

"That obvious, huh?"

She grinned. "If I may offer a little advice… Always emphasize the positive."

He looked her in the eye. "You certainly found a silver lining in what was a horrific performance today."

"It's easy to criticize," she said. "And sometimes it's deserved, but as unimpressive as Bart's performance might have appeared to you today, you would do well to remember he was trying his best."

Jim didn't like being lectured to. Never had. "His best wasn't very good."

Yet he couldn't help but marvel at this woman's always being able to find good things to say. He was also becoming increasingly aware of how good being around her made him feel, even when she was lecturing, and how she was awaking more than just physical desires and needs.

"Bart still has a lot to learn," she went on, "but the potential is there. Be patient. Just like you, he's still learning. And don't underestimate Phil Whalen. He's one of the best crew chiefs in NASCAR. If anyone can bring him around, Phil can."

They were on their way to the PDQ hospitality suite to schmooze with the last remaining sponsors and other guests when they ran smack into a group of reporters. Jim tried to veer around them, but the maneuver didn't succeed. Suddenly he and Anita were surrounded by men and women holding out microphones while the green lights on camcorders blinked.

"Do you find the parallel between you and Bart Branch ironic?" Larry Waring asked, after the predictable questions about the crash.

"Parallel?" Jim replied with skepticism. "Let's see. I have a driver's license, but I assure you I've never driven a hundred and eighty miles an hour. To be honest, the thought terrifies me. Not to mention what the speeding ticket would cost."

There were a few polite chuckles.

"No, stock car drivers are in a league of their own. I can assure you no NASCAR driver has to stay up nights worrying about competition from me."

"What I was referring to," Waring said, "was that both you and Bart Branch have fathers who are *frauds*. Ever compare notes with him?"

In the sudden stillness that followed, the reporter was actually able to lower his voice to go on. "I mean, it is true, isn't it, Mr. Latimer, that your father, Walter, spent two years in state prison for fraud? It's not on the grand scale of Hilton Branch's larceny, only tens of thousands of dollars rather than hundreds of millions, but a felony nevertheless."

Everyone had turned wide-eyed as the reporter thrust in the knife and twisted it. Their attention was refocused now on Jim whose face had darkened. He drew in his cheeks, flexed his jaw and stared straight at Anita, as if she were personally responsible for this assassination.

Anita stepped forward. "That was all in a different time

and place," she said, taking a stab in the dark, since she had no idea what he was talking about, "and frankly it has nothing to do with PDQ, NASCAR or Jim Latimer." She would have liked to give the reporter a dressing down, but cameras were rolling and she didn't want to say something that would add grist to the mill. There would be enough damage control to deal with without her contributing to it.

"Richard Latimer, a man of unquestionable integrity, as well as generosity, asked his nephew to take over PDQ Racing because of his absolute trust and confidence in Jim's ability and honesty. Let's not get sidetracked by scandals, old or new. Both Jim and Bart deserve to be judged by their own merits, not by what relatives might or might not have done."

"Are you saying Walter Latimer was innocent?" Waring asked.

"I'm pointing out that, until Hilton Branch is found, we don't know what his exact role was in the financial problems currently plaguing BMT. Folks, we're here to race stock cars. Let's keep on track." She grinned. "I'll let you decide if that pun was intended or not."

She looked into the crowd of media people, trying to gauge their mood. Avid curiosity, definitely. No question they'd do more digging. And so would she.

"Bart Branch," she continued, "is one of the best drivers in the NASCAR Sprint Cup Series. During the course of the rest of the season, you're going to see him move up."

"He didn't do very well today," another reporter called out.

She treated the observation as inconsequential. "We're still a long way from the Chase. A lot can happen by then. When he makes the cut, a new count starts."

"He's down 883 points."

She was dismissive. "From the leader," she noted. "He still has a shot at making the top twelve."

"If you examine the point spread," Jim said, back in his element now that numbers were involved, "you'll see Bart has a lot going for him."

For the next ten minutes she and Jim batted around statistics and comparisons between drivers and teams with the reporters, ever careful not to actually criticize the competition. She had to admit he'd bounced back after the initial shock and was even able to put a lighthearted tone into his replies and observations.

At last, she thanked everyone for coming and told them she looked forward to seeing them at Michigan the following weekend.

While they filed away, she checked her cell phone, or at least went through the motions of doing so.

Jim stepped up and opened his mouth to say something.

"We need to talk," she said. "Privately." She strode away without looking back.

CHAPTER TWELVE

JIM WATCHED HER WALK OFF in the direction of the grand-stands. The controlled chaos that followed every race was well underway as haulers started pulling out among long streams of cars, trucks, campers, vans and SUVs. Grand-stand elevators were disgorging seat holders as well as VIPs from the hospitality suites high above them.

Anita stepped into a vacant elevator and stood facing out, her features set. Jim followed. She was seething. So was he. She pressed the button. To anyone entering the car now, they would have appeared to be total strangers. The door closed. The cubicle rose. Jim wanted to say something, but Anita's stiff demeanor told him it wasn't time yet.

When the door opened again seconds later, he stood aside to let her exit first, as he always did. Jim Latimer, gentle-man. His uncle would be proud of him. Or would he?

They walked to the right, down an unadorned industrial corridor.

The door to the PDQ suite was propped open. Anita went in. The catering crew was in the process of cleaning up. She went to a pair of lounging chairs tucked off to the side that afforded them privacy as long as they kept their voices down.

"What the hell was that all about?" she demanded in a slow boil.

He felt like a school kid summoned to the principal's office. "Fourteen years ago my father was convicted of fraud—"

"I don't give a damn about your father," she snapped.

He was confused and doubly angry. She'd asked for an explanation and now she was refusing to listen to it. "First of all, I advise you to watch your tone, Ms. Wolcott. You're not in charge here. I am. Second, if you don't want an explanation, why did you ask for one?

"Why didn't you tell me about this before?"

"I beg your pardon?"

"You have a skeleton in the closet as big as the state pen, and you didn't bother to tell me about it."

"Why the hell should I? It's none of your damn business—or anyone else's, for that matter."

"It is now. When you took over PDQ Racing, you became a public figure. That means everything in your life and background is open to scrutiny, whether you like it or not. By tomorrow, if it doesn't make the newscasts tonight, it'll be in all the papers that Richard Latimer turned his multimillion-dollar NASCAR racing team over to the son of a convicted felon—"

"Stop right there. Did my uncle happen to mention to you that his brother was a jailbird?"

That stopped her. "No, but—"

"So it was all right for him to withhold this information from you, but I'm supposed to confess that my daddy is an ex-con?"

"I don't like surprises, Jim," she stated forcefully. Keeping her voice down only seemed to add to the intensity of her anger. "I don't like being blindsided."

"You know something, sweetheart? I don't, either. What's

more, I don't like being treated like an errant schoolboy. I know it rubs you and your friends in the media the wrong way to be left out, but I have this silly notion that I have a right as a human being to privacy, public figure or not."

"My friends?" she asked, her voice rising. "I'm not the enemy, Jim."

"Then stop acting like it."

Dead silence. Her mouth opened but nothing came out.

Heart still racing, Jim rose, moved down the balcony to the front row of theater seats, stood in front of the thick tempered-glass window and stared out at the scene below. It was hard for him to realize he owned a piece of this fantastic world. But even as he gazed out at the pageantry in front of him, his thoughts wandered back to the woman behind him. She was irritating, aggravating…beautiful and seductive…

She was driving him crazy.

She came down and stood beside him. The angle of the window didn't produce a reflection. He wished it did. He wanted to see her, but he didn't want to be obvious about it. She was right. She wasn't the enemy. At least he didn't want her to be.

"My uncle was very insistent that we work together, Anita," he said, striving to soften the tightness in his voice, "and out of respect for him I'd like to honor that request."

Was that the only reason? He wasn't being completely honest with her even now, but then maybe he wasn't being completely honest with himself, either. What he was beginning to feel for this woman went beyond professional admiration and respect. She made him too aware of his loneliness when he wasn't with her. She made him forget it when he was.

"I understand his reasoning," he continued, "and I agree

with him that we both have qualities that can contribute to a productive partnership in support of PDQ. I know *about* NASCAR. I have a good handle on the financial condition of our team, while you know your way around the NASCAR community in a way I don't."

She listened, making no attempt to interrupt. He almost wished she would. At least then he'd know what she was thinking. He wanted to hear her voice, hear sympathy and understanding. He wanted her to be not *by* his side but *on* his side.

"But I'm not going to answer to you, Anita. You wouldn't expect Richard to. I don't think you have a right to expect me to."

"Of course not," she mumbled. "That wasn't what I meant. It's just that—"

He waved her to the seats in the front row behind them. Outside, cars and people moved below them like ants, but in slow motion. He took the seat next to her and crossed one ankle over the other knee in an apparent posture of relaxation, though he felt far from at ease.

"It all happened fourteen years ago," he said quietly, "just before I graduated from State. I told you the family raises standardbred horses for harness racing. It's a tough business, a relatively narrow market, yet there's a lot of competition. People think because the sale price of an individual horse is high, the profits are, too. They don't understand the background costs, or that you're always at the mercy of circumstances you can't completely control. Horses colic, injure themselves, go lame, get kicked by other horses. The list of what can go wrong seems endless, and the expenses, I can assure you, are.

"We'd had a couple of lean years. Foals that by their blood-lines should have been champions turned out to be dolts. Sales that should have gone through easily broke down at the last minute for one reason or another. That's the way things go. People who operate highly speculative enterprises understand there will be good years and bad, and that you just have to ride them out. Somewhere down the road there'll be a turning."

Restless, he got up and paced in front of the window. "I'm going to see if there's any more bottled water left. Want some?"

"Thanks," she said without looking up.

Grateful for the excuse to flex his taut muscles, he mounted the steps two at a time and returned seconds later with two cold, sweaty plastic bottles of spring water. Twisting off a cap he handed her the drink, then sat down beside her once more.

His nerves were still ajangle, no less so from being that close to her. He would have preferred at that moment to run, to sprint, to tax his strength and endurance rather than sit quietly in a plush chair bolted to the floor. He wanted to escape this woman, who challenged him, taunted him. And he never wanted to let her go.

"Patience wasn't my father's strong suit," he said after a glug of the cold water. "He also had a tendency to cut corners when he thought no one was looking."

He took another mouthful, smaller this time.

"A year earlier," he went on, "he'd sold a very promising young pacer stallion to a woman who was looking for a good investment. Over the months that followed, the horse turned out to be a disappointment, not doing nearly as well as expected. My father convinced the woman to cut her expenses and sell the horse at a loss, which she eventually did. Two months later he approached her, having found a gelding, which he convinced her had the makings of a real champion. She bought it, and in fact the horse won the first race she entered him in at Churchill Downs."

Jim stared at the plastic bottle in his hand.

"To the casual observer one bay looks pretty much like another. Same with chestnuts. Unless they have some distinctive mark, a white star on the forehead or an odd-shaped blaze down the nose, they're all just nice brown horses to the uninitiated. In this case the two horses were unremarkable chestnuts. As I say, nice brown horses. This woman was not a true horse lover. She didn't ride for pleasure. In fact, she was a little bit afraid of the big animals. She bought them purely as an investment, nothing more, so to her they all looked alike.

"She had a friend, however, who was more discriminating. Her friend noticed, virtually at a glance, that the horse she had sold at a loss and the horse she had bought at a considerably higher price, were one and the same.

"They confronted my father, and being a smart, though foolish man, he owned up to the fraud and, thanks to Uncle Richard's financial backing, agreed to make restitution with a modest bonus added for her trouble.

"The buyer was willing to let the matter drop with that. After all, she wasn't eager to have people know she'd been suckered, but her friend wasn't as forgiving. She went to the press, and because prominent names were involved, the boys with the stubby pencils took the bit and ran with it."

Anita frowned. "So what could have remained a private matter, privately resolved, suddenly became headline news."

Jim nodded unhappily. "Before we knew it, the district attorney, who had higher political ambitions, announced he was opening a criminal investigation. In spite of Uncle

Richard's best legal efforts, the case went before a judge. My father pleaded guilty to fraud and grand theft and was sentenced to five years in state prison. He was released for good behavior after less than two."

"Where's your dad now?" she asked.

"He was never the same after that. A condition of his parole was that he was barred from buying and selling horses. The family was still willing to let him work at the stables, but as you might guess, he wasn't interested in mucking out stalls or driving horse trailers or even being in charge of grounds maintenance. He moved to California, took a series of dead-end jobs and drank most of what he earned. He's been in rehab half a dozen times since then. He's home now, but pretty useless."

"That's sad. Sounds, though, like he's his own worst enemy," Anita observed, not unkindly.

"No question about it."

"Yet you blame the press for what happened to him. Is that fair?"

"I'm not excusing what my father did. He was wrong. I can't even dispute his jail sentence. But when you get a chance, check out the *stories* they wrote about him. They brought up cases of race fixing, which my father was never involved in and for which charges were never brought. Worse were the notorious cases of animal cruelty they dredged up, incidents perpetrated by racehorse owners trying to cash in on inflated insurance policies."

Jim stared through the window at the snail's pace of traffic exiting the race-track grounds.

"My father may be a cheat and a fraud, Anita," he said with an edge in his voice, "but he never mistreated a horse.

He never intentionally hurt any animal in his life. Oh, but the reporters and commentators were slick. They never actually accused him of any of those things, just intimated that he was part of an underclass that did."

He took a deep breath, felt the helpless frustration burn inside him and fought to stanch the anger it produced.

"The family could have resolved the whole affair quietly and to everyone's satisfaction," he went on. "Restitution would have been made and a penalty paid, but the press was only interested in sensationalizing a situation. In the end they took a weak man and destroyed him. For what? The day after my father was sentenced, they dropped the matter and never mentioned it or him again. It took the family ten years to rebuild its business and reputation, and even now there are people who refuse to deal with us because of what the press said about him, about us."

Anita bowed her head. "I'm sorry."

He climbed to his feet once more, still gripping his empty water bottle, stared for another minute at the slow-moving exodus outside, then turned to face her.

"Now you know why I'm leery of the media. I know I have to deal with them, and I will, but don't ever ask me to trust them, because that's something I cannot do."

She gazed up at him. Their eyes met, locked. A long minute elapsed.

"Thank you for your candor," she finally said and got up. "I'm sorry—"

Above them they heard a small commotion, as new voices were added to the mix. Anita stood beside Jim as they both looked to the top of the balcony.

Billy stood there, Kylie Palmer and her son behind him.

CHAPTER THIRTEEN

"Hey, Dad, where you been? We were looking for you. You didn't answer your cell phone and nobody knew where you were."

Jim could hear both the panic in his son's voice and his relief at finding him. He removed his phone from its waistband holster and examined it. "Oh, um…sorry. I thought I'd put it on vibrate. In all the excitement I seem to have turned it off."

Kylie looked from Anita to Jim and back to Anita again, clearly aware that she'd interrupted something.

"No problem," Kylie said cheerfully, though, Jim noted, her eyes kept flashing concern at Anita. "I didn't really figure you'd gone anywhere." She tilted her head toward the expanse of windows looking out over a sea of barely moving traffic. "You couldn't have gotten very far anyway. It was nice seeing you, Jim. You did a great job this weekend. Your uncle would be very proud of you." She turned to Anita. "I'll swing by your office Tuesday and we can go over our game plan in the continuing saga of the Branch brothers."

"Good, good," Anita replied. Jim could see she was trying to sound positive but not quite succeeding.

"Can Ryan come over to our house when we get home and go swimming?" Billy asked his father.

"If it's all right with his mother," Jim answered, pleased that his son had made a new friend.

The two boys struck hands in a high five.

"Thanks," Kylie said. "I'll call you. Now we have to get going. You coming?" she asked Anita.

"Be right with you." Jim had invited Anita to join him and Billy on Richard's jet to and from the race, but she was already scheduled to fly with Kylie on the Branch plane so they could coordinate guest appearances by the twins. They also needed the time with the two drivers to discuss what surprises Alyssa Ritchie might have in store for them in her upcoming tell-all blockbuster about her twenty-year affair with Hilton Branch.

Kylie nodded. "I'll wait for you downstairs."

"We still have a lot to talk about," Anita said to Jim. Most of the catering staff had already departed. "Right now, though, I need to run, if I want to sleep in my own bed tonight."

The image of her stretched out between satiny sheets, her golden-red hair fanned across silken pillows, wasn't one he needed to have taunting him right then.

"We'll talk during the week," he said.

THEY WERE MUCH LATER getting home than Jim had anticipated, mostly because he wanted to supervise—correction: oversee—as many details around the track as he could. This was all new to him. It wasn't that he didn't trust people but that he wasn't sure what he was trusting them with. He went down to the garage area and watched the team pack up their cars and tools and shove off. He spent time just walking around, observing the shutdown of an operation that involved more people than the populations of many towns. He found it all simultaneously fascinating and intimidating.

He'd observed a few races from his uncle's suites over the years and seen Richard, the consummate host, gladhand a horde of guests, other owners, drivers and track officials with familiar ease. Jim had never imagined that he'd be called upon to do the same thing so soon.

He'd gotten through today without making any social gaffes, as far as he could tell, but this was sort of a honeymoon period. He was new. No one expected him to recognize them on sight. Next time they would. Conversation today had amounted to little more than endlessly repeating a report on Richard's condition and the prospects for his recovery. Everyone had been solicitous and sympathetic, but all afternoon Jim had felt like an imposter, someone playacting. Maybe one day he'd be able to handle it all as naturally and effortlessly as Richard appeared to, but at the moment, that time seemed far off.

"We're home, son," he said, gently jostling the sleeping boy after pulling into the detached garage at Richard's house.

Billy groaned, unwilling to be roused.

Jim sighed nostalgically. It seemed like only yesterday, he would have picked his son up, hoisted him onto his shoulders and carried him up to bed. He was too big for that now. In a couple of years he'd be a teenager, then a man. Now all Jim could do was jostle him, coax him to his feet and aim him like a zombie into the house, down the hall, up the stairs and into his room. Billy climbed onto his bed and curled up without ever actually waking up. Jim removed his running shoes and did something he hadn't done in a long time. He kissed him on the temple.

"Sleep tight, son," he whispered, as he closed the bedroom door and was surprised to realize there was a lump in his throat.

He should be thinking about Lisa now, thinking of the boy's mother. Instead he found his thoughts wandering to Anita, a complex woman he hardly knew.

All the way home, he'd replayed their confrontation in the luxury suite overlooking the track. There was something ironic and reassuring in her saying she wasn't interested in his father or his crimes, and in fact she hadn't asked a single question about either, not even if his father had been guilty as charged. Hell, yes, he'd been guilty. Now, hours after mulling over his blowup with Anita, Jim still wasn't sure which of them was right or if either of them was wrong.

He thought about the way the icy wariness in her eyes thawed as he told her his father's story. By the time he had finished, she might still have been angry with him for not telling her about it sooner, but her pique had been tempered by then with compassion for the shame and humiliation he and the family had suffered. Remarkably, watching her during the familiar recitation of events he'd felt his own long-held anger recede, as well. It would probably never go completely away, but the hard edges had been honed and rendered less sharp, less painful.

Something else had happened, too. He recognized that enjoying the sight of her had come to include a desire to be with her, to share her company, to share his innermost thoughts and feelings with her. She made him see the world at large differently—not through rose-colored glasses; innocence once lost can never be regained—but as more tolerant, more pleasant. With more hope. With a hunger that reminded him of who and what he was. A man.

Should he have told her about his father beforehand, so she could have been prepared?

Was he unreasonable in thinking he had a right to privacy? Not unreasonable, he'd finally concluded. Just unrealistic.

He checked his email. Nothing from Anita. Not a word. Not that there was any particular reason why there should be. He started to compose a message to her. To say what? That he was sorry he'd kept the family shame a secret? He wasn't. If he could put it in a lockbox and never let it out again, he would. That he was sorry he'd blown up at her? He was, but…

What he wanted to say was that he wished she were there with him now. That he wanted them to spend a lot more time together. Not just at NASCAR races. That he wanted them to talk about more than publicity campaigns and sponsorship programs. That sometimes he didn't want them to say anything at all, at least not in words.

He closed the e-mail and went online to do some research. He'd decided on the flight home to hire an independent accounting firm to audit PDQ's books. He'd already done the job himself, of course, so he knew everything was in order, but after the bombshell the reporter had dropped at the track, he felt it would put everyone's mind at ease about the solvency of PDQ and make sure no further accusations could be leveled against him personally. And if it did come down to him selling the team, a recently concluded independent audit would be useful.

ANITA JOINED KYLIE and her son downstairs. They walked immediately to the car Will had waiting for them to take them to the airport for the hour-and-a-half jet flight to Charlotte. She expected her colleague to question her about what had transpired between her and Jim upstairs in the hospitality suite, but Kylie made no mention of it, perhaps because Ryan was with them, and on the plane they also had no private time together. The moment seemed to be forgotten—or at least shelved for the time being.

Silence on the matter, however, and their intense discussions about the perfidy of Hilton Branch and his former mistress didn't keep Anita's mind from swirling with thoughts about her encounter with Jim.

Why had she acted—overreacted—with him the way she had? She'd been out of line, unreasonable, just plain bitchy, in her response. There was no question about that. It wasn't like her, and it made her feel ashamed. But why had she done it at all?

The answer, if it was the answer, was that she was disappointed in him, disillusioned. She had begun to feel things about Jim Latimer she'd never felt about a man, an attraction that went far beyond her respect from him as a businessman and a father—and attraction that was pure passion. Desire. A desire to share his company. Need. A need to place him on a pedestal. Neither emotion was rational, but they were true and elemental. The revelation that his background was tainted wasn't the issue. The shock that knocked her completely off balance was that he'd been keeping it secret from her and had had no intention of ever sharing it with her.

She was being unfair...unfair, foolish and judgmental. He owed her nothing. No explanation, no justification. Neither of them had made any commitments or promises to each other. They were friends, nothing more. Each of them had a right to privacy.

She'd have to make it up to him somehow.

Once the jet landed at Charlotte, nobody hung around very

long. Everyone was beat and eager to get home. She bade all goodbye and climbed into her car for the short drive home.

"Do a file search on Walter Latimer," she said into the small recording device she carried in her car for making notes to herself, as she exited the private plane parking lot.

Larry Waring had said state prison. He hadn't specified which state, but Jim had told her where the family lived.

"Check court and prison records in Tennessee."

Anita thought about Jim's reaction to the question by the smug reporter. Until then, he'd been friendly and even-handed with the media, but there was no mistaking the contempt that emanated from him at that point. To his credit, he'd recovered quickly, but the press now knew his Achilles' heel, and she didn't doubt some of them would use it when they needed to get a rise out of him. She'd have to prepare him for that contingency. Better still, she'd have to find a way to dull its sting.

She couldn't help sympathizing with him, but he was naive if he thought he could maintain privacy under the circumstances. There might have been a time when Richard could have told reporters the subject was off-limits and they would have gone along, and perhaps that was precisely what had happened, but those days were over.

It was the vulnerability, the sense of shame and helplessness she'd seen on Jim's face and heard in his voice as he told her about his father, that had captured her heart. He wasn't looking for pity or even sympathy as much as understanding and acceptance when he explained how his father had disgraced the family.

She sensed something else, too. Determination to rise above the humiliation and resolve that his own son would have a father he could look up to. Awareness of those qualities made her respect him all the more.

Maybe more than respect.

She now appreciated Jim's animus toward the press and the media. His blanket condemnation was wrong, but at least he had good reason for it, based on personal experience. She made her own resolution. To change that attitude, at least a little.

Colin Fry wrote a sports column called "Keeping on Track" in the *Charlotte Daily Herald* that was syndicated nationwide. The mug shot that appeared beside his byline showed a pleasant-looking middle-aged man. Few people realized the photo was three decades old and that Colin was closer to Richard's age than his nephew's. Maybe he would help.

Using her hands-free cell phone, she called him.

"I know this is short notice," she said, after the usual inquiry after his health and his wife's after months of non-communication, "but I was wondering if I might stop by in a few minutes to talk to you about something."

Her old friend chuckled. "I'll tell Molly to put the kettle on, and we'll all have some tea. Unless you want something stronger."

CHAPTER FOURTEEN

Charlotte Daily Herald
Keeping Track by Colin Fry
New PDQ Racing Team Owner Learned by Proxy

CHARLOTTE, NC—PDQ Racing's new owner, Jim Latimer, learned a difficult lesson fourteen years ago when his father was sentenced to prison after pleading guilty to fraud and grand larceny. Walter Latimer, younger brother of PDQ founder Richard Latimer and Jim's father, served two years in the state penitentiary back then for his role in a horse-selling swindle.

When asked what he thought Jim took away from his father's terrible ordeal, an associate said, "The meaning of the old adage that honesty is the best policy, that cheating doesn't pay. It may sound corny," admitted the source, who wishes to remain anonymous because he does not represent Latimer and is not authorized to speak for him, "but it's true. Jim has learned from his father's painful experience that honor and personal pride are priceless."

Indeed, despite this background, Jim Latimer himself became a highly regarded and very successful independent certified public accountant before his uncle, legendary NASCAR owner, Richard Latimer, asked him to take over the NASCAR Sprint Cup Series team.

"I trust him implicitly," Richard is reported to have said when asked about his choosing his nephew to succeed him as owner of PDQ. "There was never any question in my mind that Jim was the right man for the job. He loves NASCAR, and his integrity is beyond reproach."

When asked his reaction to learning that his team owner was the son of a convicted felon, Bart Branch, NASCAR Sprint Cup Series driver of PDQ's car No. 475, remarked that it made absolutely no difference to him. "I know firsthand," he said, "that we are not responsible for other people's actions. I have the highest respect for Jim for moving on with his life. He's an inspiration, because that's exactly what I plan on doing with mine."

Branch's father, Hilton Branch, former head of the Branch Mutual Trust, is currently being sought by authorities for the disappearance of an alleged quarter-billion dollars.

JIM READ THE ARTICLE TWICE. It was on the same sports page as Larry Waring's snide column in which he tooted his own horn for uncovering the unsavory truth about Walter Latimer. Jim's emotions had risen and fallen with each twist of the reporter's sharp pen. They seesawed with Fry's article, too, but the overall effect was quite different. He had no doubt who had furnished the quotes supposedly made by his uncle. There was no way Richard could have said what he supposedly did to the reporter. If ever Jim needed confirmation that the media and the people associated with it were frauds, this was it. Yet...

He picked up the phone and hit speed dial.

"I'm just wondering who the anonymous source is who quoted Uncle Richard," he said when Anita answered. He didn't bother to identify himself.

"You don't think the sentiments are accurate?" she asked with what sounded like smug amusement.

"He never said those things, and in his present condition I doubt he could."

"Are you sure? I don't recall the article specifying when the statements were made. Maybe he talked to Fry before he had his stroke."

"Slick. I'll have to give you that."

"You're not suggesting that I'm the source referred to in the article, are you?" By her tone one would think the very notion was preposterous.

"Aren't you?"

"I believe it referred to that person as he, not she."

Jim snorted. "Since Fry got other things wrong, he could have gotten your sex wrong, too." As if anyone who saw or heard her would have any doubts she was a woman.

She had the audacity to laugh. "Gee, Jim, you do wonders for my self-esteem."

He refused to take the bait. "Great cover, though. Like I said, 'slick.'"

There was a pause on the other end, followed by a huff. "Tell me, Jim, what do you think the objective of that article was?"

"Does it make any difference?"

"To you, I guess it doesn't. Do you have Sandra's number in your directory?"

"What?"

"Sandra Jacobs, the head of Motor Media Group. My boss. You are obviously displeased with the way I'm handling public relations for PDQ. I'm sure if you give her a call, explain to her that I've perpetrated a fraud—for which, you might add just to be fair, you have no proof—she can assign someone else to handle your account."

"My, my, aren't you thin-skinned this morning." He couldn't help smile as he said it. There was something very satisfying in getting under her skin. He didn't for a moment doubt, despite her denial, that she was behind the news piece…although, come to think of it…she hadn't actually denied it, either, only said he couldn't prove his allegation. A jury would have to bring in a verdict of not guilty. That didn't mean, of course, that she was innocent.

No words came from the other end, but he could visualize her pretty face, mouth pinched, those beautiful green eyes set with determination.

"Why don't you come to dinner this evening?" he asked.

"What?"

"I can't promise gourmet cooking, but it'll probably be edible."

A momentary pause, then she chuckled, clearly relieved that the tension between them seemed to have dissipated. "Edible, huh? Gee, with an enticement like that, how could a girl possibly resist? What time?"

"It's Monday, your day off. Why don't you come by around four and bring your swimsuit. We have a pool. We can go for a dip before dinner. In fact, you can come earlier—"

"Four is fine." There was mirth in her voice now.

"Um, one other thing," Jim added. "Do you like pizza? That's my usual fallback position."

She laughed this time, an unselfconscious explosion of joy that surged through him like an electric charge. "I have a feeling this afternoon is going to be interesting," she said.

Very interesting, he agreed.

ANITA STOPPED BY THE HOSPITAL to visit Richard, Monday afternoon. In spite of grueling therapy, he still had no use of his right arm or leg, and the seventy-three-year-old was clearly discouraged.

"Hang in there," she told him sincerely. "I suspect you'll make progress in plateaus, like climbing up mountain terraces."

He nodded. Speech was still very difficult for him, too. He mispronounced and slurred words, spoke painfully slowly and much too loud. "Tell…Po-co-no." *Tell him about Pocono?*

She gave him an honest but not-too-detailed description of the weekend.

"Jim… How…?" *How is he doing?*

"Fantastic," she said and reminded him how well Jim had done in the news conference, which Richard had seen, insisting Jim had a natural rapport with the media.

"W-Waring."

"Oh, you saw that." But of course he would have. TV was about all he had now. He couldn't use the phone. Couldn't write. Reading was very difficult. But he could flip the television remote with his left hand just fine.

"Good quote," he said, "from me in paper."

She felt more than a little sheepish and avoided his eyes.

"Good job," Richard added.

She looked up and saw him giving her a lopsided grin.

"You…him?"

It took a moment for her to understand what he was asking, and when she did she felt even more uncomfortable. He was asking how she and Jim were getting along. Jim had pointed out that his uncle wanted them to be a team, but the heated exchange between them yesterday was anything but that.

"We're doing fine." She laughed. "In fact, he invited me over to your house for dinner tonight."

Richard made a sound that she recognized as a chuckle. Forcing the words out, he said, "Pizza. Burns burgers."

She laughed heartily this time. "Jim told me pizza would be his fallback position. He didn't say anything about burning burgers."

They talked a little about the race. Richard didn't seem in the least bothered by Bart's crash. Anita wished his nephew was as patient and forbearing. Maybe with time.

As if a cloud had passed in front of the sun, blocking out the light, the elderly man suddenly appeared exhausted. She gave him an affectionate kiss on the cheek, told him to get some rest and left feeling almost lightheaded.

"NO…B-B-BURN…BURGERS," Richard strained to say.

Jim examined the card attached to the latest bouquet of roses, amber this time, on the table near the window. Aunts Vi and Ethel, and Jim's mother, Julie. Walter's name was on it, as well, though Jim wasn't sure his father had anything to do with this or any of the other deliveries that had been arriving every week. The three women had visited only once, then had returned to Tennessee and their families. Walter hadn't been by at all, though he had sent a promise that he would visit.

"Burn burgers?" Jim repeated, and wondered if his uncle's mental capacity might not have been affected by his stroke after all. "I'm sorry, Uncle Richard. I don't understand."

"He's saying not to burn the hamburgers tonight when Anita comes over for dinner, Dad," Billy explained.

His uncle grinned, pleased the boy could so easily figure out what he was trying to say.

"Ah." Jim laughed. "So she's already been here, has she? I should have known she'd beat me to the punch. She warned me she has a tendency to be early."

"Good…weekend?"

"I met Carl Edwards, Uncle Rich," Billy dove in, unaware that the question had been directed to his father. "He told me how to tell Will and Bart Branch apart. I haven't had a chance to test it yet, though. And I met this other kid. His mom works for Will Branch like Anita works for Bart. He likes to play soccer and he's really good. Dad said it'll be all right for him to come over to swim in the pool."

"Ryan Palmer," Jim explained. "Kylie's son. Seems like a nice kid."

"Is," Richard agreed. "B-B-Bart?"

Jim put a bullish spin on their driver's performance, repeating Anita's assertion that he'd been moving steadily up until the unfortunate crash and subsequent pileup.

"Op-timist," Richard said.

Jim wasn't sure who he was referring to, him or Anita; if he was concurring with the assessment or mocking it.

"She certainly believes in a positive approach," he agreed. "Always looking for the silver lining."

"Tonight…burgers."

"Yeah, yeah," Jim said with a happy chuckle. "Don't burn the burgers. I've already warned her we may have to send out for pizza."

"She told Dad she likes pizza," Billy contributed.

Richard awarded them one of his crooked smiles, and Jim was sure he saw a twinkle in the old man's eye.

On the drive home, Jim couldn't stop thinking about Anita and their "date" tonight. Did her telling Richard about it mean it was important to her, too? Or was he reading too much into a casual remark, made perhaps in a lull in the conversation with a man who had to strain to say every syllable?

At the house, he and Billy worked as a team preparing for their dinner guest. Jim formed six generous hamburger patties, though he supposed his son was the only one who would even consider eating two. Billy skimmed the swimming pool of leaves.

A car pulled up in the driveway and came into view through the kitchen window.

"She's here. She's here," Billy yelled from the backyard.

Jim glanced at the NASCAR clock over the sink.

Yep, she was early. He had to stifle a smug grin of satisfaction.

Swinging the kitchen door wide open, he stepped out into the afternoon sun. She started getting out of her car. No business suit for her this evening. No stylishly casual outfit with long sleeves for the track. One long, bare, well-shaped leg emerged, followed by the other. She was wearing a pair of lime-green shorts and a white tank top, exposing more of her skin than Jim had seen before. The sight was definitely pleasing to the eye. Jim's heart did a thump.

"I'm a little early," she acknowledged, as she reached

back inside the car to remove a canvas carryall. "I hope you don't mind."

It wasn't his mind but his libido that was being affected by the sight of her beautifully shaped rear as she leaned over.

"We've been waiting for you," Billy said. Not a chance for subtlety with that kid, but then he wasn't seeing the woman the way his father was.

"Come on in," Jim said, surprised he didn't have to clear his throat to get the words out.

His hand brushed hers briefly, as he took her bag. She smelled like cool, spring flowers. Billy made himself useful by slamming her car door for her. Both adults jumped.

"Not so hard, son," Jim cautioned him, though his eyes remained riveted on Anita.

She smiled and he nearly dropped her tote. They could have gone through a door in the backyard fence directly to the pool area. Instead Jim suggested they detour through the kitchen and get a cold drink first.

Was it his imagination or was she as ill at ease as he felt?

Billy led the way. Jim placed her bag on a stool by the counter separating the kitchen proper from the breakfast nook where he and Billy ate their meals. They went through the ritual of getting drinks. She opted for iced tea with lemon, like Jim's. Billy was drinking fruit punch that left him with a burgundy mustache.

They talked about their trips home. That took all of two minutes.

"You went to visit Uncle Richard today," Jim commented, adding a sprig of spearmint to both the special acrylic glasses Lisa had given Richard for serving outdoors. They had a matching set at home but had never gotten around to using them. A fleeting frisson of guilt snaked through him at the thought of her, but was gone the moment he handed one to Anita and their fingers touched. "He said we missed you by about half an hour."

"He seems to be coming along all right," she remarked.

He heard the tentativeness in the statement, as if she weren't sure it was true and wanted confirmation. "Much too slowly," he said. "He's frustrated." But he wasn't eager to discuss frustration. "Ready to go swimming?"

"I've been looking forward to it all day."

So had he. At the moment, though, he was having difficulty not staring at the thin pale blue straps of her bathing suit peeking out from under her white tank top.

He waved toward the door beside the bay window. Billy went first, prattling on nonstop about playing soccer that morning over at Ryan Palmer's house. They moved onto the veranda and faced the shimmering reflection of the sun on the pool. Jim ushered her to the right, to a green, wrought-iron table and cushioned chairs, shaded by a beach umbrella.

"Did you bring a bathing suit?" Billy asked.

"I have it on." She pulled her tank top out of the waistband of her shorts and lifted it over her head.

Jim sucked in a breath as his eyes beheld her bare, sculptured midriff, then her bikini top. She kicked off her sandals, then tucked her thumbs under the waistband of her shorts and started to tug them down.

Jim stopped breathing altogether.

"Aren't you going swimming with us?" she asked, her eyes questioning why he was making no move to take off his T-shirt and shorts.

Suddenly the idea of shucking his outer garments in front of her seemed like a very dangerous thing to do.

"You bet." He sat on the edge of a chair and started to unlace one of his canvas topsiders, though he usually just slipped his bare feet out of them.

He kept stealing glances at her long, smooth, perfectly shaped legs.

"Come on, slowpoke," she teased, smiling down at him.

He had a feeling from the gleam in her green eyes that she knew exactly what he was thinking. That she was enjoying his discomfort wasn't nearly as important as the fact that she seemed okay with the thoughts themselves.

He should have had a smart comeback, but he didn't. The notions going through his brain weren't the kind that lent themselves to words. Besides, his lips were too firmly trapped between his teeth for intelligent sounds to escape. Not when she was standing only a few feet in front of him in only a light blue bikini. Not just wearing it, filling it out. Definitely filling it out. Not too much. Just enough to keep his pulse racing and his blood pooling. *Grrr.*

She laughed, then turned and jumped into the pool, splashing water onto the deck and his bare legs. He pulled his shirt over his head, stepped out of his shorts and dove in after her.

The cool water helped, but what he really needed, he decided, was an ice-cold shower, though he wasn't even sure that would calm him.

Clearly oblivious to what was going on, Billy retrieved a bright red-and-orange vinyl pool ball from the edge of the cool deck and proposed a game of volleyball.

"You and me against Dad," the boy said, "'cause he's really good."

"How do you know I'm not really good, too?" she teased.

"As good as Dad?"

She grinned and shrugged. "Probably not." She looked over at Jim who was treading water in the deep end. "You up to it?"

He almost swallowed a mouthful of chlorinated water. "I'll give it my best."

CHAPTER FIFTEEN

ANITA HADN'T MISSED the look on Jim's face or the gleam in his eyes when she was getting out of her car or later as she was taking off her clothes. It was a strange and pleasurable feeling to be admired, to be—dare she say it—lusted after.

She supposed she'd always been aware, at least on the intellectual level, that she possessed certain feminine qualities. She'd felt eyes following her across rooms from time to time, but there was something different about the way Jim looked at her.

Sexual interest? No question about that. But was there more? Or was the hunger she saw in his eyes only a reflection of her own desire, of her need?

What surprised her was that Jim didn't seem to realize he was having a similar effect on her. She hadn't fully appreciated what a physically impressive man he was. He could have done commercials for one of those home gym machines with his broad, thick-muscled shoulders, well-defined chest and rippled belly. Was he really as oblivious of his image as he seemed? She'd never known him to put on an act. He was too serious for that.

She watched him jump and dart as she and Billy batted the ball to him. Billy was right. His dad was good.

"Okay, I'll say it," she finally called out an hour later. "*Uncle.* You guys are too much for me." She panted through a wide grin. "I haven't had this much fun in ages."

A few minutes later, they all climbed out of the pool. Jim tossed her one of the thick, fluffy towels from the pile on a side table.

"I'll light the grill," he said. "We can eat out here, if you like. Won't have to get dressed, if we do. Or we can go inside. Might be a bit chilly in the air-conditioning with no clothes on. Er…"

Anita glanced over at Billy who had run around the other side of the pool to snag the ball. He was too young to understand sexual tension. But she wasn't. The idea of sitting across from that bare, nearly hairless chest lent a whole new meaning to appetite.

A mosquito buzzed. She slapped at it and missed.

"The bugs are coming out," she said, holding his glance. "I vote for inside. With our clothes on."

"Spoil sport." He rubbed a dark green towel over his head to dry his hair. The sight of his upraised arms flexing with the vigorous motion was downright mesmerizing, and for a moment she stopped breathing. That kept happening around him.

"Come on, Billy," he called out a moment later. "It's time to set the table."

She liked watching father and son go about what was obviously a routine. Billy put the plates on the table and lined up the silverware. He allowed her to fold the dark blue cloth napkins—the cloth being a concession, he admitted, to having a guest for dinner—and put them lengthwise on the china plates, while he got out the condiments: ketchup and mustard, mayonnaise, sweet relish and dill pickles, and lined them up in the middle of the table. The setup was more formal than she would have expected for a couple of guys, especially when the menu was hamburgers, but she decided she liked the sense of ritual, of order. The boy's father was, after all, an accountant. A place for everything, and everything in its place.

It came as a bit of a shock when she realized that Jim reminded her of her dad, though why he should she couldn't say. They certainly didn't look anything alike. Her father had been blondish with blue eyes and fair skin. Jim Latimer had jet-black hair, dark eyes and a tan complexion. Maybe the response went back to their first meeting at the hospital, when she'd bumped into him—the way he'd held on to her to keep her from falling, the way he'd steadied her, his protective strength and confidence.

"Tell me about your uncle," she said when they finally sat down to eat, determined to break away from thoughts that could easily become obsessions. "I really don't know anything about him, except that he made his money in the stock market."

Jim seemed to relax. He loved his uncle and it showed. He glanced at his son, who was eating heartily, but also listening intently.

"Richard was the eldest of four children. He has a brother and two sisters. As I understand it, he'd just graduated from high school when their father died in one of those accidents that should never have happened—fell off a roof is what I've heard. So at eighteen, Richard became the man of the house and quickly learned that, while they had a socially prestigious name and owned considerable property, they had barely enough cash to pay the taxes on it. Turned out the garden and livestock he always thought of as his mother's hobby was in fact their main source of food."

Billy asked if he could have another hamburger. As the boy was fixing it, Jim continued.

"Richard passed up the scholarship to Harvard he'd earned for a job as a runner for a stockbroker. It didn't pay much, but it did keep the tax collector from their doorstep. He was smart and took full advantage of the opportunity to learn the business, especially the volatile commodities and futures markets. By the time he was twenty-five, he'd amassed enough money to send his brother and sisters to prestigious Ivy League colleges and pay someone else to tend his mother's garden."

"Never married?" Anita asked.

Jim shook his head. "According to my aunt Vi, he was engaged to a young lady of considerable beauty and talent when he was in his early twenties, but she died of some sort of fever a couple weeks before they were to be married."

"And he never fell in love again," she mused. "How sad, and how poignantly beautiful, too."

"She must have been quite a woman," Jim agreed.

"Everything was absolutely delicious," Anita said an hour later, as she leaned back in her chair and patted her belly.

The meal was as simple as it had been orderly. Hamburgers, baked beans and a huge garden salad, a relish tray of pickles, onions and sliced tomatoes, all followed with strawberries and ice cream over shortcake.

"And nothing was burned," she added.

"You only have to burn burgers once," he said with feigned indignation, "to get a reputation."

"DAD, I KNOW WHAT I want to be when I grow up," Billy announced.

Jim looked over at Anita and winked. "An accountant, of course, just like your old man." He studied his son's somber face and laughed. "Not."

Billy squirmed, not wanting to alienate his father by saying no, but even less enthusiastic about saying yes.

"So what do you really want to be?" Jim asked casually. "A race car driver?"

The boy's face lit up. "How did you know?"

Jim had to smile. Didn't every kid want to be a fireman or a policeman or a race car driver at some point? "Call it a lucky guess."

"So can I?"

"I think you can become just about anything you want to be, son. You're a little young, though, to get behind the wheel of a NASCAR stock car. You may have to start out in something a little smaller."

"Well, sure." The boy was leery, as if agreeing to this was some kind of trick.

"There's a go-kart track not far from here," Anita observed. "That might be a good place to begin."

Billy stared at her with deep gratitude for her support. "Can I, Dad? Can we go there now? Please?" He jumped up and down, then raced to the kitchen. "Let's go." Seconds later they heard the door to the garage slam.

"A fine mess you've gotten me into this time, Anita," Jim mimicked, grinning widely.

"You know about the Charlotte Juniors, don't you?"

The Charlotte Junior Driving Club had been organized more

than twenty years ago to teach kids from six to sixteen how to drive sport vehicles in a controlled and safe environment.

Jim nodded. "I was wondering how long it would take him. I already checked. I can get him in the new group of ten-to-twelve year olds next week."

Anita smiled happily and patted his cheek. "You're a sly one. Didn't say a word."

"I figured I'd better be prepared. Let's see how well he does with the go-karts tonight before we say anything. He might drive like a granny."

She laughed. "Yeah, right."

Billy didn't. He was too aggressive the first time, too cautious the second, then he seemed to settle into concentration mode. He was fearless through it all, but thanks to the safety measures they had in place, Jim felt relatively unafraid. Squeezing Anita's hand as they watched Billy zoom around the track seemed perfectly natural, comfortable. He wanted to ask her if she felt the same, but he was afraid he would break the spell.

"It's a good thing we've already had supper," Anita observed. "I'm not sure how he would be able to eat with that grin plastered permanently on his face."

"He's a boy," Jim replied. "He'll eat."

LATER, SITTING AT THE GAME table in the den, hovering over her dominoes as she contemplated her next move, she was drawn back to a time that constituted a small but important segment of her life, the years when her father was alive and her mother was a vibrant, energetic young homemaker. When they were a family. She couldn't remember ever playing dominoes with them, and she was sure they'd never gone to a go-kart track. But there had been board games, jigsaw puzzles and Chinese checkers on the card table her mother set up in the living room, and trips to the miniature golf course. Those years before her father died had been too few, but they had also been the happiest of her life, a time of unconditional love and carefree security. She could have grown bitter when they ended. There had certainly been moments of depression during her mother's long, slow physical decline. But the moods were fleeting. For the most part, she looked back on them for inspiration and inevitably found it.

Now with his mother gone, Billy was facing his own loss of innocence. Anita gazed over at Jim and felt encouraged. Billy had a loving and conscientious father to guide him, a good role model to emulate. If the boy harbored resentment and anger for the loss of his mother, he had it under control.

The grandfather clock in the hallway had already struck nine-thirty when Jim finally told his son it was time for him to go to bed.

"Do I have to?" Billy whined uncharacteristically, surely a telltale sign that he had finally run out of steam.

"Yep," Jim said easily. "Tomorrow's another day."

It took a little more prodding, but then the boy went off to brush his teeth. When he returned to say good-night to Anita, he came over and gave her a quick, impulsive hug. Then, with a jerk, as if he'd just realized what he'd done, pulled away.

Trying not to react to his abrupt withdrawal, she told him how much she'd enjoyed the evening.

"Will you come back?" he asked.

"If you'll let me."

He nodded.

Father and son disappeared upstairs.

Anita wandered around the spacious room, examined Richard's collection of fiction in the bookcase along one wall—mostly thrillers and mysteries—and the big globe, dated now that so many countries had changed names or redrawn themselves. As she passed behind the desk to examine some of the framed photos on display there, she noticed the writing on the pad by the telephone.

Taney.

The name of a fellow team owner shouldn't surprise her. There were any number of reasons why he and Jim would have talked. It could be nothing more than Taney calling to congratulate Jim on his taking over PDQ.

That was probably it.

Except that it had been rumored for some time that Will Branch's team owner was looking to expand and was shopping around for another established team to buy.

Jim had told her he was exploring ways for his uncle to economize. It was possible, she supposed, that he had called Taney to discuss the feasibility of a particular approach. But why Taney? There were so many other owners who could give him sound advice. The answer, of course, was obvious. Will Branch. If Jim was going to collaborate with someone—or offer to sell the team to someone—Taney would be the logical first choice.

She moved over to the windows looking out on the side garden. Discreetly placed landscaping lanterns cast it in a soft, unfading twilight.

Jim had talked about replacing Bart as his driver. Surely he wasn't considering selling the entire team. Richard would never stand for it. Unless Jim was anticipating Richard not pulling through. Jim wasn't yet comfortable in the owner role, but that was natural. He needed to give himself time. Like his assuring his son there wasn't anything he couldn't do if he set his mind to it. she couldn't imagine Jim being unable to handle whatever challenge presented itself. He wasn't a quitter.

She was still contemplating the peaceful garden when the man came downstairs a few minutes later. He moved up behind her and placed his hands on her shoulders. The intimacy of his touch sent a tantalizing ripple of warmth through her.

"Thank you for joining us this afternoon," he murmured, "and for going with us to the track."

"Thank you for inviting me, Jim." She rolled her shoulders under his soothing touch, savoring the feel of his strong hands and the affection she heard in his voice. "I thoroughly enjoyed it. It's been a long time since I felt like I was part of a family. You have a great kid."

He massaged her shoulders, a slow, gentle application of pressure. "I think he's infatuated with you."

She had to smile at that. "You think?"

"He takes after his father."

All at once she felt afraid to be alone with this man. Not afraid of *him,* but fearful of her own reactions to him, unbalanced by the tension rippling undeniably through her, flowing between them. They'd been alone together before—in offices, in work areas—but that had been for business. This was private and dangerously personal.

"It's the red hair," she quipped, acutely aware of how close he was standing behind her, near enough for her to bathe in the heat emanating from him. "Turns men's heads."

"Indeed it does," he whispered into her ear.

With those same strong hands, he turned her around so they were facing each other, only inches apart. For an interval that might have lasted a second or an hour, he continued to hold her, and they gazed into each other's eyes.

As if it were the most natural thing in the world, she caged his hips with her arms. His fingers slipped across her shoulders, bracketed her neck. He cradled her head between his hands as he brought his mouth down to hers. Their lips touched. She heard a soft moan and realized it was her own. He deepened the kiss, and she let him, welcomed him. Oh, she'd been kissed before, but not like this, not in a way that made all else—time, place, him, her—disappear.

When at last they broke off, they continued to hold each other. Her pulse was racing. Her skin tingled. It took all her strength to separate herself from him, not because he wouldn't let her go, but because she didn't want him to.

"Don't leave," he objected. "Not yet."

"I have to."

"Stay a little longer." It sounded like a plea, a plea she wanted so much to grant.

"I have a long day ahead of me tomorrow," she said, moving on rubbery legs toward the doorway.

When she reached the foyer, he took her hand, spun her around so that they were again facing each other.

"I wish you didn't have to go," he murmured. "Can't tomorrow wait?"

I'm afraid, she almost blurted out. *I don't know what's happening and it scares me.* But rather than boldly acknowledge what she really wanted, she tried to make light of it.

"Tomorrow waits for no man…or woman," she jested,

not sure what she was saying, what it meant, if it even made any sense.

He didn't laugh.

Instead, he leaned forward and brought his lips to hers again. Some part of her mind must have told her to pull back, but more primitive instincts and long-denied needs over-ruled it. When he wrapped his arms around her once more and deepened the kiss, she melted into it.

"I have to go," she murmured. "I have to go."

He nodded and slowly blinked. Forgetting he was a gentleman, he stood there and watched her open the door for herself. "This time," he murmured. "I hope not next time."

Panic flooded through her. "See you at Michigan."

Her last sight of him was his dark, powerful presence silhouetted in the doorframe, as she pulled out of the driveway.

They had crossed a threshold, breached a barrier, glimpsed a vantage point from which nothing would ever look the same.

She hoped with all her heart she hadn't made a mistake.

CHAPTER SIXTEEN

HE HAD JUST DROPPED HIS SON off and was on his way back to his uncle's house to review more of the voluminous files Richard had stored there, when his cell phone chirped. The caller ID spelled out Gideon Taney.

"I'm in town for a couple of days before going up to Michigan, and I was wondering if you might have a few minutes available today or tomorrow for us to get together and talk."

Jim was tempted to ask about what, but of course he knew. A meeting between the two NASCAR owners in public, including Jim appearing at any hotel where Taney might be staying, was bound to stir media speculation. After a brief exchange, Taney agreed to come to Richard's place later that afternoon.

"Can I get you something to drink?" Jim asked when his guest arrived exactly on time.

The tall, solidly built man accepted a soft drink, and the two of them settled down in Richard's spacious den, surrounded by the collection of trophies and awards that PDQ's owner had accumulated over the years.

Taney got directly to the point. "I'm interested in expanding Taney Motorsports' presence in the Sprint Cup Series," he said. "And as you might have guessed, I'm looking at PDQ as a good place to start. Bringing the two brothers together would be a big draw PR-wise."

"A good reason for me to buy you out," Jim countered lightly.

"If you were buying and I were selling."

"What makes you think *I'm* interested in selling?"

Taney smiled indulgently. "The fact that I'm here for one."

Jim had to laugh. "I should have seen that one coming." He paused for a moment. "To be perfectly honest, Taney, I'm in no position to make such a decision. Not right now, at least. Depending on how much my uncle's health improves, I may well be turning control back over to him. That's what I'm hoping. As things stand right now, even if I retain control, I'm not going to sell without his blessing. I think you can understand that."

Taney nodded. "Of course I do, and I respect it, but things don't always turn out the way we want or anticipate. I'll be blunt, Jim. I know PDQ has had a couple of lean years financially. I also know sound fiscal management—for which you have an excellent reputation, by the way—isn't going to put it solidly in the black. It's going to take a few years of the kind of aggressive, experienced know-how about NASCAR that doesn't come quickly or easily. It's not contained in books."

Jim wasn't sure he'd ever been knocked down with more finesse or civility.

"Let me lay another card on the table for you to consider," his guest went on. "I know your major sponsor, EZ-Plus, is not an enthusiastic partner, and that they are, shall we say, squeamish about the upcoming bad publicity surrounding

Bart's old man and his mistress when her book comes out. Whether justified or not, the moral issues work against their staying on with you next season, especially in light of Bart's erratic performance on the track so far this year."

Taney had not brought up the brouhaha that was already in the newspapers and on sports shows almost every day about Jim's father's criminal background. Because it didn't matter, or because it was powder he was keeping dry until they got into serious negotiations? Either way, Jim respected him for not raising the subject, though the father-son parallel was inescapable, if not implied.

"Bottom line? I just want to remind you—" Taney got up and extended his hand "—that if you do actively consider selling, I'm definitely interested."

JIM AND HIS SON ARRIVED in Michigan via Richard's private jet late Thursday afternoon. Sitting in the back of the chauffeur-driven limo his uncle had reserved in advance, Jim called Anita on his cell phone on their way to the race track, hoping she'd be able to meet them there. On the second ring, she answered in a whisper, saying she was involved in a media promotional happening and wasn't able to break way.

Her sultry voice made him take a deep breath. "Come by the motor home later," he said, "and have dinner with Billy and me."

"Charred burgers?" she asked with a chuckle. Her voice was more stable, suggesting she'd stepped out of whatever meeting room she'd been in, but it still sent an electrical charge short circuiting his system. "The last batch weren't too bad, come to think of it."

"So you'll come?" he asked hopefully.

"I wish I could, but this thing is going to keep me tied up all evening. Let me take a rain check."

He was disappointed and told her so.

"Me, too, but my client is a real slave driver. He'd get me fired if he found out I passed up a big promotional opportunity to eat burned burgers with some guy I hardly know and his really cute kid."

"The jealous type, huh?"

She laughed. "I'll see you in the morning in the garage area."

Father and son went to their motor home. Jim had started researching other coaches for trade-in, either for him and Billy, or for Richard. If his uncle was ever able to travel again he'd most probably need one with handicap features. There were a variety of possibilities, all with price tags that would make any accountant stutter.

"I'm hungry," Billy said, the minute they stepped inside.

Jim chuckled. Of course he was. "There's fruit and yogurt in the refrigerator. Fix yourself a snack."

After a banana and two containers of yogurt, Billy was ready for his next priority: hooking up with Ryan Palmer. This prompted Jim to call Kylie, who predictably was at the same meeting with Anita. Ryan, she reported, was at the soccer field just beyond the owners' and drivers' lot, kicking around a ball with a dozen other kids.

Billy, now the proud owner of his very own cell phone, went to join them, and Jim made his way to the garages.

Phil Whalen greeted him familiarly and several other team members waved or nodded. The noise level was already high enough to make ordinary conversation at close quarters difficult. At longer distances, it was impossible.

"This track is going to be a test of smarts and stamina," the crew chief stated as they watched a mechanic adjust a carburetor setting.

"Rather than skill and daring," Jim said. "Yes, I know."

The race track, located not far from Detroit, the home of the American auto industry, was a classic D-shaped oval and at first glance didn't seem like it would be much of a challenge. The roadway was wide, the turns not particularly sharp. Banking was well-designed. The front stretch was also one of the longest in the NASCAR Sprint Cup Series, yet there was no restrictor-plate mandate, which meant cars reached, and sometimes exceeded 180 miles per hour.

"Bart'll do all right," Phil assured Jim. "for some reason everything feels right this weekend. The pit crew is in top shape, and we've tuned that engine to within a nanometer of its life."

"I hope you're right. If he finishes in the top ten, I'll be happy," Jim said. "Don't tell him that, though. I want him focused on Victory Lane."

Phil gave him a strained smile. "Bart's good, Jim. Still a bit rough around the edges, I grant you, but he's got the stuff." That was a strong endorsement, but then Richard would never have taken Bart on if he hadn't thought the same thing.

It made Jim wonder, though, what kinds of rumors might be floating around that Phil felt he had to make that statement at all. Had Anita let slip some comment that the new owner was considering dumping his driver? Jim doubted it. Whatever disagreements they might have, he didn't think she would betray what he'd made clear was a confidence. He could probably chalk it up to everybody expecting change when a new owner took over a business.

"And he's got the best team in the world backing him up," Jim said. "I know that, too."

The crew chief's smile this time was more genuine.

THE FOLLOWING AFTERNOON, Bart took seventeenth place in the starting lineup, which wasn't great, but it wasn't bad, either. It would put him in the lead pack. As he'd pulled onto pit road after the qualifying lap, however, he complained about running loose on Turn Four, even though in practice laps he hadn't had the problem. Running loose meant his rear-end traction was poor.

"Understandable," Jim commented to Anita later. "In his qualifying lap he was pushing harder than he had been during practice. The problem is that he should have been pushing harder in practice, finding out where the break point was."

"It was cooler during practice yesterday than it is today," she reminded him. "A few degrees in temperature can make a big difference."

Which was certainly true. Even a thin layer of clouds coming over a track during a race could change its dynamics. A hot track was more slippery than a cool one because the asphalt was softer. Conditions could change not just from day to day but from hour to hour, from lap to lap.

For the race on Sunday, the weather was not just cloudy, there was intermittent drizzle. Weather conditions were always a consideration, and rain inevitably caused problems. Races were scheduled years in advance; concessions and tickets were sold months, even years, before the event. A slip in the timetable by even a few hours had ripple effects that could be enormously costly, not just to owners, their teams and drivers, but to spectators and fans, as well. However, the final arbiter, in the end, was always safety.

"What's the word?" Anita asked Jim, after he received his second telephone call from track officials.

"No delay. We're racing."

"I'm not sure if I'm happy about that," she admitted. "Bart hasn't had much experience on wet tracks."

"The consolation is that the same can probably be said for half the field."

For fans it was really good news. Spinouts were more likely. Rarely did a car lose control without impacting other cars. A speed race then turned into an obstacle course. Fans certainly found it exciting to watch, and drivers ate up the adrenaline rush, but for owners and crew chiefs it was yet another problem to worry about.

"If he's going to get experience on wet pavement any-where," Anita commented, "this is as good a place as any."

As expected, the first laps were slow. Average times were almost three seconds below normal. Over the initial twenty-seven laps, four cars, three of them driven by rookies, lost control going into Turn One because they were going too fast after the long front straightaway. The first car hit the wall and bounced back into the pack, causing a four-car pileup. The second car did a spectacular roll and was ultimately eliminated, while the third lost two laps because of body damage, but still managed to finish the race. The fourth car produced a riveting "slide show," as it skidded sideways for more than half the length of the front stretch and ended up hunkered down in the muddy grass of the infield.

Bart almost lost it on lap sixty-seven, but then the sun came out and conditions quickly changed. He moved up three positions, then three more. He was passed by two cars, yet managed to overcome them four laps later.

Three-quarters of the way through the four-hundred-mile race, he got clipped on the backstretch coming out of Turn Three. He lost six positions that time, but managed to recover five of them in the next twenty laps.

He finished in eleventh place. Not as good as Jim would have liked, since he missed the top ten, but considering the circumstances and the manner in which he handled himself, Jim was pleased, and when he got to see Bart in the garage area later, he told him so.

"I should have moved up sooner," the driver said with uncharacteristic humility.

"You can indulge in the coulda-shoulda later," Jim told him and patted him on the back, "and I'm sure you'll learn a lot from going over the reruns. But right now, I want you to know I think you ran a damn good race."

"Thanks. I appreciate that."

"That was nice of you," Anita said, as they were taking the golf cart under the track to get back to the stands, so Jim could say goodbye to the last departing guests in his uncle's hospitality suite.

He glanced over at her. "You don't have to sound so surprised."

"Does that mean you're reconsidering your decision to let him go at the end of the season?"

"You're jumping the gun, Anita. I haven't made any such decision. It was an option for my uncle to consider. That's all it's ever been. Today has been just one race. There are plenty more ahead." He maneuvered around a group of people. "I will say this, though. If he continues to show the kind of concentration and professionalism he showed today, I'll keep him on, regardless of his final ranking for the season."

CHAPTER SEVENTEEN

HOME IN MOORESVILLE, JIM continued to work his analysis of PDQ's fiscal position. His uncle had always been a savvy businessman, his rags-to-riches success was proof of that, but his most recent investments made Jim wonder if Richard's mental state might not have been slipping for some months without anyone realizing it. Jim would have liked to discuss the matter with him, to see if there could be something he was missing, some cunning investment strategy he didn't see, but he seriously doubted it and decided that this was not the time to question a man struggling to perform the most ordinary of activities of daily living.

Jim unloaded eight of Richard's most recent stock-market purchases, two of them at a significant loss, two at modest profits—which was pure luck, because a week later they plummeted—and the remaining four at break-even. The transactions also added cash to their dwindling reserves. Jim had known intellectually that NASCAR was a big-buck business, but until he found himself in the position of personally signing off on six- and seven-figure transactions, the full reality of it hadn't sunk in.

He kept thinking about Taney's offer to buy PDQ. No specific dollar amount had been quoted or even suggested,

and Jim felt certain cutting a deal would be a very complicated process. The idea, however, had definite appeal. It
wasn't that he didn't enjoy NASCAR, that he didn't take
pride in being a team owner or that he wasn't honored to
have his uncle entrust the last twenty years of his life's work
to him. Aside from the time-management issue he had mentioned to Anita, Jim wasn't sure he was up to the challenge.
He hated to say that, even to himself. He'd never been a
quitter, never given up on anything without a fight, but being
a team owner wasn't a game, the outcome of which didn't
matter. Running a NASCAR team had a tremendous impact
on a large number of people.

It was still much too early to actively pursue that option,
but at the point where his temporary caretaker status became
permanent ownership, he would have to give selling very
strong consideration.

The next weekend race Jim was able to get to was at
Loudon, New Hampshire. At the team meeting on Thursday
evening, Phil Whalen addressed the challenge ahead.

"No significant changes since the last time we were here,"
he informed the assembled group, standing in front of a screen
displaying a graphic presentation of the race course. The
Loudon track was similar to the one at Martinsville, a tight
one-mile oval with sharp turns, only moderately banked, and
long straightaways. Passing was extremely difficult on the flat
stretches and virtually impossible in the turns, all of which
made winning the pole especially important.

Lots were drawn Friday morning to determine the order
for running qualifying laps that afternoon. The winner of
the bingo-style ping-pong ball selection process wasn't
given the first crack at the track, but was allowed to choose

when he wanted to drive his lap. The number two winner then chose his slot and so on. Running later rather than earlier in the qualification process was preferred because it gave the driver the advantage of observing the drivers ahead of him and learning from their performances. Unfortunately Bart's number was so high that he had little choice in the matter.

"Dang," Jim said when the pecking order was finally announced. Bart was second in the qualifying lineup.

"You can't blame a guy for blind chance," Anita reminded him.

"I'm not blaming him," Jim countered in a tone of annoyance. "But a break would have been nice."

When the actual race starting positions were announced later that afternoon, Bart was in the twenty-first position in the field of forty-three.

"Look at the bright side," Anita said. "He's in front of more than half the other people on the track."

Jim laughed. "You don't give up, do you?" He had to admire that.

Through his practice laps Saturday morning, Bart kept complaining of traction problems. Phil and the team adjusted everything they could think of and a few combinations they hadn't considered before. Finally, Bart declared success.

"It's going to take a month of Sundays to figure out what we've done right," Phil declared later that evening, when he put the car to bed and told everyone else to do the same.

Sunday was slightly overcast, which meant a cool track—and a fast one. It wasn't rainy, so the pavement was also dry.

Passing on the long, narrow straightaways was difficult

but not impossible, and by the hundredth lap, Bart had moved up eight positions. Jim was already calculating—at that rate of advancement Bart had a good chance of actually winning the race. That was probably unrealistic, however, given the caliber of the competition still in front of him, so Jim computed more conservatively. The most promising outcome was that Bart might gain another eight positions overall. That would move him to the number five spot. Jim would be pleased with anything in the top ten.

Bart lost one place on lap 115, but then regained it five laps later. The race was going well.

He was in twelfth position by lap 256, when he tried to challenge Jem Nordstrom on the backstretch. Nordstrom, to nobody's surprise, wasn't having any of it. With no one on the inside close enough to challenge him, Nordstrom slipped right as Bart moved up on the outside.

"Fall back," Phil advised him over the radio.

They were both going hell-bent toward Turn Three.

"Fall back," Phil repeated, more adamantly.

Going into the turn abreast simply wasn't feasible. The curve was banked only twelve degrees, not enough to hold ground at those speeds.

"Pull back," Phil insisted a third time, but Bart seemed determined to play chicken with his opponent, ignoring the fact that Nordstrom had never gotten high marks for playing well with others.

Nordstrom held the middle ground all the way to the turn, then cut left to hug the clear inside lane, tapping his brakes at the very last fraction of a second. He held the curve.

Bart slammed into the wall.

At first it appeared that it wasn't going to be more than

a fender bender, that Bart would scrape along the outside wall through the curve and proceed, relatively unimpeded, into the front straightaway.

The pack behind him had already started to negotiate Turn Three single-file below him. He fought to maintain control as he slid and bounced against the shock-absorbing outside barrier, until one of those bounces tossed him into the flow of traffic.

Suddenly he was spinning.

Then he was being battered.

Tail. Hood. Tail.

He spun around twice more, slipped into the inside lane where he was again clipped.

This time the forces attacking him conspired to send him rolling on the grass island between the track and pit road. Once, twice, three times. Four.

He came to a standstill upside down, momentarily lost in the swirling smoke from scorched tires.

The yellow caution flag had gone up. People in the stands were on their feet, and it was as if they all let out a collective gasp, then subsided into silent staring.

Rescue vehicles were already on their way. Crew members wearing fire suits were running from every direction toward the smoke-shrouded vehicle. Motion slowed to a crawl.

"Bart, speak to me," Phil said into his mouthpiece.

"I'm all right," came a deceptively calm voice.

"Help's coming," Phil said. "Hang in there."

"Like hell," Bart said.

A moment later, as the trucks came to a halt, a figure emerged from the overturned stock car.

A sigh of relief akin to laughter exploded from the grandstands.

Once completely clear of the wreck, Bart joined his gloved hands above his head and twirled around to let everyone know he was all right.

Jim wasn't sure his heartbeat would ever return to normal.

HE AND ANITA MET MONDAY at noontime in his uncle's hospital room. Richard had watched the New Hampshire race on TV. He was happy Bart had escaped his crash and disappointed he hadn't finished the race, but seemed not at all upset that a car worth a quarter of a million dollars had been destroyed.

"He's getting expensive to keep around," Jim remarked, trying to make the comment sound offhanded, wondering what his uncle's reaction would be. "This is the second car he's destroyed this season."

"He seems to crash only when you show up," Anita said, the gleam in her eyes making it clear she was teasing him.

Richard rattled off a long mumbled stream of indecipherable sounds. Jim and Anita both turned to the therapist who had been there when they arrived.

"He says you shouldn't be racing if you can't afford to replace cars," the middle-aged therapist explained.

Jim wished he could understand his uncle as easily as this woman and Billy seemed to. There were so many things he wanted to talk to his mentor about, so much advice he would have welcomed. At the same time, this statement made him wonder anew if his uncle realized or perhaps didn't remember the cash-flow pinch the team was experiencing.

"Bart has a lot on his plate right now," Anita reminded

him. "That's not an excuse, but it might help explain his impulsive need to prove himself."

After they left Richard's room, Jim asked, "How have Bart's guest appearances been going? Any…attitude problems?"

She shook her head. "None. He's always prompt, courteous and in good spirits. Give the guy some slack, will you? Under the circumstances I would expect you to be more sympathetic."

He frowned. "I learned a long time ago, and he's going to have to learn soon, that self-pity is a luxury nobody can afford. But enough about Bart Branch for the time being. My concern at the moment is these sponsorship proposals I'm receiving for next year. They're all low. Maybe that's normal procedure. I just don't know. This is all new ground for me. Negotiating deals was something my uncle thrived on, but—"

"Maybe I can help."

He perked up. "How?"

"I told you I started working for Sandy part-time when I was in college. One of my administrative duties was taking notes at meetings with clients, especially those involving contract issues. I don't claim to be an expert, but I did pick up a few things."

"That would be great." His cell phone vibrated. He looked at the display. "It's Billy. I'd better take this."

She nodded. He walked over to the window as he put the instrument to his ear.

"Dad, when are you coming to pick me up?" He was spending the afternoon at the Palmers', kicking a soccer ball around with Ryan.

Jim glanced at his watch. "In about an hour. Why?"

"Could you come sooner?"

"What's the matter, Billy? Is something wrong?"

"Mrs. Palmer wants to talk to you."

A moment later Kylie was on the phone. "Jim—"

"Is Billy all right? Has something happened?"

"He's fine," she assured him. "But there was a little incident. He was in a fight."

"I'm leaving now," Jim said. "I'll be there in twenty minutes."

"WOULD YOU LIKE ME TO DRIVE?"

Jim snapped out of his trance, realized he was drumming his fingers on the steering wheel and stopped long enough to look over at Anita. "What did you say?"

"I asked if you want me to take the wheel. You're so keyed up you're making me nervous."

She heard Jim inhale deeply and let the air out. The light turned green and he pressed down on the accelerator.

"Sorry," he said. "I'm fine, really. It's just that…Billy had some problems with temper tantrums after his mother died. I hoped moving here might break the pattern. He seemed to be doing so well. I was beginning to think Uncle Richard and the therapist were right, that he just needed a change of environment, to get away from constant reminders of her."

"I was at about his age when my dad died. It's hard for children to fathom death, Jim. Hard for any of us. Be patient with him. Billy's an intelligent, healthy boy. He'll get through it. Time is a great healer."

Grunting lethargically in agreement, he drove north toward Lake Norman and Mooresville. Kylie and her son lived with Kylie's widowed mother in an upscale area of Lake

Norman, not very far from Richard's house. Mature, towering trees lent a comfortable, settled atmosphere that was very appealing. Jim pulled up in front of a two-story, steep-gabled house. He switched off the engine. They got out.

The front door opened before they reached the top step.

"It wasn't my fault," Billy declared, standing in the shadowed doorway, his hand still clutching the inside knob. He had a scrape on his right cheek and the left side of his upper lip was discolored and swollen.

"Are you all right?" Jim asked, as he studied him.

"He's fine," Kylie assured him from inside. "Hi, Anita."

She nodded. "Hi." Like Jim, her attention was on the boy. "What happened?"

"Come on in," Kylie beckoned, at the same time she motioned Billy to go back inside. "I'll get you some tea, and he can tell you all about it."

Anita looked behind her friend and saw Ryan standing on the lower step of the staircase, his hand on the newel post. He appeared unscathed.

Everybody filed through the living room to the kitchen in back. Jim and Anita were invited to sit at the table by the window overlooking the neatly trimmed yard. Beyond it was a stand of tall, dark-green pines. Kylie poured two glasses of sweet tea and checked the boys' plastic mugs for refills of fruit punch.

Once she joined her guests at the table, Jim asked Billy for an explanation of what had happened.

"It wasn't his fault," Ryan volunteered. "Honest, Mr. Latimer. This kid, Garth—"

"No one was talking to you, Ryan," his mother cut in sharply. "Mr. Latimer asked Billy to explain."

"But—"

She gave him a look that Barbara Bush would have been proud of. The boy instantly clammed up.

Meanwhile Jim continued to stare at his son.

"Me and Ryan were—"

"Ryan and I," Jim corrected him.

Billy lowered his head and took a breath. "Ryan and I," he emphasized, "were kicking around the ball when this other kid, Garth…"

"Hollister," Ryan contributed.

"Yeah, this big kid, Garth Hollister, came over and started kicking it away from me. I figured he just wanted to get in on the action, so I played along. He's big, but he's slow and dorky. The first time I got the ball away from him, he didn't say anything. The second time he elbowed me. I called him out, told him he fouled me, but he just ignored me. Really made me mad."

"Billy told him to back off," Ryan put in, then remembered he was supposed to keep quiet. He let the last word drop to a murmur.

"He got a shot off to Ryan," Billy continued, "who returned it. Nice kick, too," he said to his friend who grinned happily, before he realized he shouldn't. "That's when I moved in. I mean he's open, right? Like standing there, waiting for the ball to come to him. So I kicked it back to Ryan. That's when Garth runs up and butts me from behind, yelling it was his ball. I started to laugh, so I didn't see him swing. I ducked just in time. Well, almost." He touched his tender cheek. "That's when I walloped him."

"A good one," Ryan added enthusiastically. "Garth got

really mad, reared up like some kind of fat old bear or something and jumped on top of Billy. I ran over—"

"Let Billy tell it," Kylie instructed him, enumerating each syllable.

"Oh, yeah. Sorry."

"I clobbered him, Dad," Billy said proudly. "He took another swing and I gave him everything I've got. Right in his big, fat belly." He snickered. "It was like hitting a sponge ball, 'cept I hit his belt buckle, and cut my hand." He gazed at the bandage across the middle knuckle of his right hand. The skin around it was red and puffy. "That was the worst part. Really hurts."

"Ryan called me on his cell phone," Kylie elaborated. "Said the cops were on their way."

CHAPTER EIGHTEEN

"COPS?" JIM'S EYES WENT wide with shock. "The police were called?"

"They weren't," Kylie clarified, "but Garth's mother—I know Erleen from church—had run over when the fight began and was threatening to call them."

"She was worried her big fat baby was hurt," Ryan sing-songed with contempt.

"Ryan—"

"He's a wimp, Mom," Ryan objected. "You should have seen him crying on her shoulder like he was going to die or something when all he got was a black eye. Deserved it, too, the fat doofus."

"Ryan, what have I told you about calling people names?"

"Doesn't count if it's true," he answered back, then froze when he realized what he was doing. He slinked into silence.

Kylie awarded him that measured look that only mothers can produce. "We'll talk about this later, young man."

Cringing, he muttered, "Yes, ma'am," just above a whisper.

"So except for a scratched cheek, a fat lip and a cut hand, you're all right?" Jim asked his son.

"He didn't really hurt me," the boy claimed with stalwart bravado, forgetting that just a moment earlier he was looking for sympathy for his wounds.

"And he was the one who threw the first punch?"

"I just told you, Dad."

"It was Garth, Mr. Latimer," Ryan added. "Really. It was him who swung at Billy first."

Jim wondered. The boys seemed awfully eager to convince him this other kid had started it all. Still, Jim hadn't been there, and neither had Kylie, and from the impression he was getting about the other boy's mother, he didn't think he was likely to get a reliable answer from her, either. It came down to the classic case of one boy's word—actually two boys' words—against another's.

"If that's the way it happened, fine," Jim said.

"It is, Dad," Billy assured him, his expression hopeful. "You always tell me I can't throw the first punch, but if somebody else hits me I should hit him back hard enough to make sure he doesn't want to do it again. That's what I did."

Jim rubbed his chin.

"Don't worry about Mrs. Hollister," Kylie told him. "She's more talk than action."

Kylie then told Ryan to say goodbye to Billy, Mr. Latimer and Ms. Wolcott, and go up to his room. She'd be there in a few minutes.

The boys shot a high five. "Cool, dude," Ryan said. "Bye, Mr. Latimer, Ms. Wolcott."

"Thank you for helping Billy," Jim responded.

A little sheepishly, the boy nodded and slowly began to climb the stairs, looking back once at his friend.

Kylie walked her guests to the front door.

"Thank Mrs. Palmer, son," Jim said, "then get in the car. We'll be out in a minute."

Billy didn't argue. He looked uncertainly at Anita, said

a polite thanks to Ryan's mom and walked down the path, shoulders rounded at first, then, with distance, he squared them, marched on and climbed into the backseat.

"I'm not totally convinced we got the whole story just now," Kylie said. "I'm going to have another talk with Ryan."

"Thanks for stepping in and handling the situation. I'm very grateful."

She shrugged. "Boys will be boys, Jim. I don't think we're going to change that. I'm not even sure I want to."

"If Ryan tells you anything different from what they just said, will you let me know?"

"Sure thing." She placed her hand on his forearm. "Don't worry about Billy, Jim. He's a good kid. Ryan needs to take a short break to reevaluate the error of his ways, but then Billy is welcome over here anytime."

Jim drove Anita back to her office.

"It's practically quitting time," he said, pointing to the dashboard clock that said it was nearly five. "Why don't you pick up your car and follow us home. Join us for dinner."

"Yeah," Billy said from the backseat. "Come eat with us."

She mulled it for only a few seconds, tempted to tease him about burned burgers but figured that subject, or rather non-subject, had been pretty well beaten to death.

"Tell you what," she replied. "I still have a few things I need to clear off my desk, then why don't I come over and bring pizza?"

Billy's face lit up.

"Sounds like a plan," Jim said. "Billy and I will be having a further discussion when we get home about what happened." Billy's face fell. "How long do you think you'll be?"

"Shouldn't be long," she said.

He raised an inquiring eyebrow. "So how long is not long? An hour? Two hours? Three?"

"Ah, the bean counter." She laughed. "Wait, let me get out my calculator." She reached for her bag. "Let's see, forty-two seconds to get upstairs, file six pieces of paper at one-minute, thirty-four seconds each—"

"A rough estimate will be fine," he said, using humor to disguise the edge of annoyance in his voice.

"An hour?" she asked, as if to confirm that would be acceptable. "If I'm going to be any longer, I'll call. How's that?"

He chuckled. "Why is it always so hard to get a clear answer out of a woman?"

"It isn't. It's getting the answer you want from a woman that's the challenge. You won't believe this, but we have the same problem with men."

"Yeah. All you want us to say is we love you, while we want to count the ways."

She drew back and cocked her head, a grin slowly lighting up her face. "My, what an interesting analogy."

"Maybe we ought to explore it further later."

"Maybe we should," she agreed.

"What kind of pizza?" Billy asked from the backseat. They both laughed.

"What kind would you like?" she inquired.

"Pepperoni and sausage with three kinds of cheese."

"Oh, my arteries." She groaned.

"We'll have an extra-healthy salad to compensate," Jim consoled her.

It was almost two hours before she actually showed up, but true to her word she had called ahead, at the one-hour point, to say she was going to be delayed.

As a consolation prize, when she did finally arrive, she brought not one but two pizzas. Pepperoni and sausage with three kinds of cheese, and a spinach and feta.

"I decided we needed antioxidants to round out this gourmet repast," Jim told her as he put out the huge bowl of salad greens and a collection of bottled dressings. "Billy is having unfermented New York State Concord. I thought we might have a California vintage." He produced a bottle of grape juice for Billy and a Cabernet Sauvignon for them.

"A true connoisseur," she declared.

They all sampled the two pizzas. Billy even allowed that the spinach one *wasn't bad.* Then they all pitched in to clear the table. Finally, they played the card game Uno until it was time for Billy to go to bed. He protested, of course, but not very hard, perhaps because he wasn't completely sure if he might be in the doghouse for the day's events.

He thanked Anita for the pizza and playing cards before going up to his room. She realized how good it felt, this feeling of family.

A few minutes later, Jim came back down.

"How about some more wine?" he asked. They'd had only one glass with their meal.

She would have enjoyed another, would have liked to lounge and talk and sip—and maybe go a step further.

"I better not," she said. "I have to drive home."

"Coffee then. I have decaf."

"That'd be nice. If you don't mind."

They returned to the kitchen. She sat on a stool on the other side of the counter, while he set the coffeemaker to hissing and gurgling.

"How was the talk with Billy about the incident today in the park?"

"He's sticking to his story."

"You don't believe him?"

He shrugged. "It probably didn't happen exactly the way he and Ryan say it did, but I think it was pretty close."

"What do you mean?"

"From what I can figure, Garth probably didn't throw the first punch, but I have no doubt the kid was bullying him. Pushing his weight around, so to speak."

"And that makes it all right with you?"

He looked at her. "All right? Makes what all right?"

"Fighting."

"No, it's not all right, Anita, and I reminded Billy of that. I certainly don't encourage my son to go out and start fights, but if he's attacked, I'd be disappointed in him if he didn't stand up for himself."

He removed a pair of shiny black mugs from an overhead cabinet and set them on the counter, then took spoons from a drawer and placed them beside the mugs.

"I gather you disagree," he said.

"I guess I would have handled it differently is all."

He leaned the back of his narrow hips against the opposite counter, close to the coffeemaker, which was filling the room with a rich, tantalizing aroma.

"How would you have handled it then? Or advised Billy to deal with the situation?"

She didn't hear a challenge as much as mockery in his question. "I would have advised him to avoid further physical contact."

"Run away?"

"Is this typically male, posing two opposite extremes, flight or flee? Do men never see a middle ground, a gray zone?"

"You haven't answered my question."

"Not run necessarily, but back off, get out of the other person's reach and try to find out why he did it?"

Jim paused for a few seconds, his lips moving in and out. "Someone has just punched you in the face, and you stop to ask him why he did it?"

She said nothing.

He crossed his arms over his chest. "And if you did ask him, what difference would the answer make?"

The sight of his shirt pulled tight across his shoulders and upper arms instantly evoked a recollection of his bare, shiny wet torso at poolside. She really didn't need such distractions. "I don't understand. What do you mean?"

"Is there an acceptable explanation for him punching you in the face?"

"There could be."

The machine stopped grumbling and sputtering. He removed the carafe from the hot plate, brought it over and filled her cup. "Name one."

She thought about it for a second. "Maybe he didn't mean it."

"Not credible, Anita. There's only one reason for a person swinging his fist in the direction of someone else's face. I've never heard of anyone attacking someone's knuckles with his nose." He grinned. "Try again."

She frowned.

"Maybe…" She started to wrap her hands around the steaming mug, then realizing how hot it was, withdrew them. "Maybe he thought the other guy had taken a swing at him and was reacting."

"Good," Jim said, after filling his own cup and returning the pot to its stand. "You just agreed with me that it's acceptable to throw a punch in response to someone else's violent aggression."

Her frown deepened. This wasn't going the way she wanted. "I just don't think fighting is good."

"It's not a matter of good. It's a matter of necessity. Give away the right of self-defense and you've given away all your rights, including your right to live."

She completely disagreed. His answers were too pat, too simplistic. Not every problem could be solved with brute force. What about negotiation and compromise? She wanted to tell him he was missing the unique qualities of reason and understanding that make people human, but she didn't want to argue with him. In the end she doubted either would convince the other. Nothing would be accomplished except their disagreeing.

"You're probably right," she said, essentially practicing what she preached by backing away from a fight. She sampled the coffee. Its invigorating taste matched its aroma.

As he gazed over at her, she was surprised at the disappointment she saw in his dark eyes.

Because she'd conceded his point? Refused to dispute it further?

She was a little disappointed in herself, too. Sorry she'd given in so easily.

CHAPTER NINETEEN

THERE WAS A MYSTIQUE ABOUT Daytona. One of the longest tracks in the NASCAR Sprint Cup Series—only Talladega was longer—it was prestigious because it was the oldest. NASCAR had begun on the hard-packed sand of Daytona beach. Winning there lent a certain credibility to any driver's résumé.

Six months into the racing season the spread between the leader and the twelfth-place driver was less than seven hundred points. Bart Branch was trailing by over a thousand. The gap between him and the driver in twelfth place wasn't insurmountable point-wise, but it was a formidable challenge because he had to contend against other drivers who were equally intent on getting ahead.

By now, Billy was at home in the infield, and Jim was comfortable letting the boy search out his new friends. The cell phone was one reason. Jim knew he could find the boy whenever he wanted or needed to, and Billy was good about obeying the rules Jim had established. He knew he'd lose his privileges if he didn't. For his part, Billy was ecstatic about the amount of freedom he had when they were at the track. The only thing better would have been going into the garage and pit areas, but the rules forbade anyone under eighteen from those places.

Because Daytona was so special and had such a party atmosphere—some fans showed up more than a week ahead of the race weekend—Jim and Billy arrived on Wednesday afternoon instead of their usual Thursday. Billy had brought his soccer ball, so his first priority was finding Ryan Palmer and the other kids they played with.

The air was redolent with the tangy aromas of charcoal fires cooking everything that could possibly be grilled: steaks, chops, hot dogs, hamburgers, chicken, sausage of various kinds, as well as beef and pork ribs. Country music blaring from boom boxes competed with rock and gospel. The country-fair atmosphere was infectious; people walked around unconsciously sporting smiles on their faces and talking with total strangers as though they were old friends.

BILLY, RYAN, THREE OTHER boys—and one girl—had formed two teams and were playing a lively round of soccer, when Carl Edwards passed by. Billy immediately stopped action to call out to him.

"Hey, Billy." Carl returned the greeting with a toothy smile as he ambled over. The other kids, wide-eyed and awestruck, closed ranks around him. Billy, their instant leader, made the introductions. His best friend, Ryan, then Chad, Sam, Elliot and Mia.

"Will you kick the ball around with us for a while, Mr. Edwards?" Billy asked.

"Sure looks like fun, but I don't want to interrupt your game."

"Maybe we can reorganize," Chad suggested.

"How are we going to do that, genius?" Elliot scoffed.

"With Mr. Edwards, we have an odd number now. Unless you want to drop out."

Chad wrinkled his brow and screwed up his mouth. "Heck no."

"Maybe we can find another grown-up to make the sides even," Sam proposed.

"And who is that going to be?" Mia asked with the practiced sarcasm of a woman three times her age.

Carl looked around, saw someone he knew, raised his hand and called out, "Hey, Larry. Professor Grosso."

A tall, lanky, middle-aged man, wearing neatly pressed cream-colored chinos, a black T-shirt and red-and-blue Maximus Motorsports cap, turned to face him. He had been striding past on long legs in the direction of the grandstands, where scattered spectators were watching practice laps. He stopped, pointed to himself and mouthed, "Me?" Then he recognized Carl and grinned.

"Hello, Carl." He came over. "You playing soccer now?"

"We're short a player. How about joining us?"

"I'm tall, but I'm not very good." Nobody seemed to notice the short-tall pun.

Carl introduced all the players to Professor Larry Grosso. "He's Steve Grosso's father. Steve is a spotter for his cousin, Kent Grosso."

"Kent Grosso drives car No. 427," Billy volunteered.

"That's right," the professor said, clearly pleased that his nephew was known.

"He's in eleventh place, a thousand and twenty-seven points behind the leader," Billy continued.

"You're absolutely correct, young man. Oh—" he glanced at Billy "—did you say your name was Latimer? I bet you're related to Richard Latimer, the owner of PDQ Racing. So you're here to cheer for Bart Branch." He scratched his head. "Seems to me I just saw him with his brother going somewhere a few minutes ago." He narrowed his eyes in thought. "Now where was that?"

"Can you play with us, Professor?" Sam asked impatiently. "Then the sides will be even."

"Well," he said slowly, "as I told you, I'm really not a soccer player. Basketball's my game. And swimming. But if it'll help, I'm willing to give soccer a try."

"Yay!" two of the boys sang out.

"You can play on Ryan's team," Billy offered. "I want to play with Mr. Edwards."

"Hey," Ryan objected, "I thought the prof here was going to play on your team."

"Nah." Billy dismissed the idea. "You're better than me. You can carry the professor here better than I can."

The personage in question cast Carl an amused expression.

"I am?" Ryan asked, astonished at the sudden praise. He puffed out his chest. "Well, yeah, I am, but…" Being recognized as a better player was something to be desired, but it obviously also came at a price.

"Sure," Billy insisted smoothly. "You won the last two games."

"It was only by one point," Mia reminded them with a scorn-filled scowl, "and that was only because Sam screwed up the block."

"No, I didn't," Sam objected. "It wasn't my fault."

"Guys," Carl interrupted, holding up his hands, "I hate to put any pressure on you all, but I don't have a lot of time before my team meeting. Do you think we can get started?"

"Sure, Mr. Edwards," Billy said, cheerfully taking charge again.

Passersby, recognizing Carl, were beginning to gather along the sidelines to watch. The first play went quickly foul, but the second lasted several minutes. To everyone's delight, the two teams turned out to be fairly well matched. The professor ran around like a puppet without strings, all elbows and knees, yet before anyone realized it, he was the first one to score a goal. Billy pulled off the second point on a smooth rebound from Carl.

The game picked up momentum as they learned to judge each other's skills and weaknesses, and an increasingly larger, enthusiastic group of onlookers began clapping and cheering.

Mia fell on her butt when she kicked the ball so hard it flew directly between the professor and Ryan, who dived for it but missed. Having made the goal, she picked herself up, dusted herself off and gave Ryan a smug grin.

Carl and Billy each gave her a high five.

By then his dad and Anita had shown up and were standing on the edge of the crowd, cheering as boisterously as everyone else. A minute later, Anita was on her cell phone.

The score shifted to five to four in favor of the professor's team.

"Come on, Mr. Edwards," Billy called out. "We can't let them get away with that."

"Looks like the cavalry has arrived," someone yelled out and pointed.

Everyone turned to see the Branch twins approach, matching smiles on their identical faces. They were dressed alike in faded jeans and running shoes, except each wore his respective team T-shirt and baseball cap.

"Pick your sides, guys," Carl called out.

Bart, wearing the PDQ red and orange, naturally chose Billy's team, while Will in black and silver, joined the professor's boys.

They played for another twenty minutes, each side scoring two more points. That still kept the professor's team ahead by one point.

Carl called a time-out so they could huddle to devise a strategy. Within a minute of resuming play, Billy and Carl had worked the ball to their end of the field while Bart, Sam and Mia played defense.

Carl shot the ball to Billy.

Wham! Billy slammed it past Ryan, where it hit the corner of the net post and rolled inside.

Excited cheers went up.

Carl raised both arms, then pointed down to Billy to give him the credit. More cheers and hoorahs. Billy had never felt so great in his life.

"A good place to stop," Carl said a minute later. "You guys are awesome. You ought to try out for the Olympics."

He shook all the players' hands, saving Billy's for last. "Nice kicking, kid. You can be on my team any time."

"Thanks for playing with us, Mr. Edwards. That was awesome," Billy said, as the others crowded around, jumping up and down. "You were cool."

"You're really good, too, Will," Ryan told his teammate.

"Yeah," Billy agreed and tossed him the ball. Will caught it with his left hand. Billy looked at Carl and they both smiled.

"Go on. Tell them," Carl said with a conspiratorial wink.

Billy couldn't control the broad grin on his face. "Except that's not Will, it's Bart."

Everybody exploded in derisive laughter.

"Look at the team colors they're wearing, kid," an older man called out.

Billy shook his head. "He's Bart." He pointed to the driver in the Taney Motorsports T-shirt and cap. "See, Will is right-handed, Bart is a lefty, and he just caught the ball in his left hand, so he's Bart."

The two brothers put their arms on each other's shoulders. "I think we've just been made, bro," the one wearing the PDQ shirt said.

"You mean the kid's right?" someone asked in astonishment.

"Yep," the twin wearing Taney black and silver agreed, then exchanged hats with his brother. "Gotcha all."

They laughed and the crowd roared with them.

"How did you figure it out?" Mia asked Billy.

"Carl told me the secret when we met at Pocono, but I didn't have a chance to test it until now. I saw the fake Bart heave the ball only once, but he did it with his right hand. I couldn't be sure he wasn't just trying to fool me. I had to make him reach for the ball when he didn't have time to think. That's what I just did."

"Slick," Ryan said approvingly.

His dad came up behind Billy and placed his hands proudly on his shoulders. "Nice going, son." In an obvious gesture of approval, he said to Bart, "I may have to make you sign something before I let you climb through the window from now on. Something like a check, just to make sure you are who you say you are."

Everybody laughed again.

Bart spun around and finally saw Anita. "You can thank her. She called me on her cell to let me know there was a game underway. I'm glad she did."

"It was fun," Will agreed. "Maybe we can do this again sometime."

"You'll have to practice more, though," Bart ribbed him.

"Speak for yourself. I was the one who got a goal. You didn't."

"That was just luck. In my case…"

The two brothers waved to the cheering crowd as they hurried toward the garage area, still arguing about which of them needed more practice.

"I have to go, too," Carl announced. "Thanks for a great afternoon, guys."

"Thanks for telling me the secret," Billy said, his face still beaming.

"My pleasure. You handled it like a champ. Maybe some day you can share a secret with me."

Everybody applauded as he trailed behind the twins on his way to the garages.

CHAPTER TWENTY

"WHAT THE DEVIL IS HE doing?" Jim muttered, as he peered through his binoculars.

It was Sunday at Daytona. He and several dozen of his uncle's closest friends were in the PDQ hospitality suite, high above the stands watching the four-hundred-mile race in cool, quiet comfort. The aromas of the lavish buffet, set out for guests to snack from while they imbibed adult beverages and soft drinks, mingled with the perfumes of the women present. Some were stylishly casual in their attire, others were coiffed and gowned as if they were at a Hollywood premier. No one wore jeans or T-shirts, except the small children who ran around playing tag and hide-and-seek, oblivious to the cars circling the D-shaped track beyond the wall of windows.

"I was hoping you could tell me," Mark Jessup said as he bit into a bacon-wrapped barbecued shrimp, one of half a dozen on the gold-rimmed white china plate he was holding.

Bart was in eighteenth place, having started off in ninth, and the race wasn't even at the halfway point yet. He had tried three times to pass Dean Grosso on the outside, but the thirty-year veteran had other ideas. One of the oldest drivers in the NASCAR Sprint Cup Series, Grosso had been doing reasonably well this season—at least until this race. He'd had to start in the number thirty-one slot because of a carburetor problem in his qualifying lap. His engineers seemed to have fixed it; the No. 414 car was performing well and Dean was moving steadily forward, but he still had more than a dozen cars in front of him.

"Maybe he's looking for another Lucky Dog win," Mark suggested with a hint of sarcasm.

Jim liked to think of himself as an easy-going sort of guy. He certainly wasn't normally inclined to form a negative opinion of a person on their first meeting. He made an exception to that rule, however, in the case of Mark Jessup.

The second thing that struck Jim was that Jessup made it clear he was not a NASCAR fan.

"Why is EZ-Plus a sponsor?" Jim had asked Phil Whalen when they talked that morning.

Whalen had shaken his head and snorted. "Your uncle and Raymond Salas, the president of EZ-Plus, are contemporaries. When Richard approached him about sponsorship after the Hilton Branch debacle, Salas was happy to accommodate him, but then he turned the details over to his promotions people, unaware apparently of this guy's attitude toward NASCAR."

"Richard must have been pretty desperate to put up with the likes of Jessup." The man emanated negative vibes from the get-go, making Jim wonder how he had ever come to be a VP at the internationally successful software company.

Whalen signed the bottom of a form on the clipboard one of his mechanics had presented. "He was a lot more tactful around Richard, almost fawning at times. I'm sure he knew, if your uncle complained about him, there would be hell to pay."

Salas had come to visit Richard at the hospital. Unfortunately, it had been at a time when Jim wasn't there. He would have liked to have met the man, not that he was inclined to go complain to him that his VP was a jerk, but being able to say they had met might have altered Jessup's attitude a bit.

It was also clear that Jessup had a particular dislike for Bart Branch.

"Any idea why he hates Bart?" Jim had asked Whalen.

The crew chief had shrugged. "I don't know for sure, but there's a rumor going around that Jessup's father was heavily invested in BMT, and that his retirement portfolio took a major hit when the stock's value came crashing down."

Now it all made sense.

It was an indication of Richard's desperation for a sponsor, any sponsor, that he had agreed to Jessup's conditions that the sponsorship contract be at a reduced rate and that the renewal for the next year be contingent on Bart's performance this season. The real problem, in Jim's estimation was that Bart's record so far was erratic. He was almost a thousand points behind the leader. Without Richard at the helm to cajole and arm-twist, what were PDQ's chances of holding on to this reluctant sponsor or finding another?

Jim picked up the bottle of imported beer he'd been nursing for the past hour. He usually enjoyed this particular brew, but today it tasted bitter, and now it was warm. He watched Bart, driving car No. 475, pass No. 468, driven by Mitch Volmer, on the inside. Volmer was down one lap because of a blown tire. Bart then tried to pass car No. 452, driven by rookie Clyde Coogle, on the outside of Turn Three. It was no good, however, and he was forced to fall in behind him.

Bart stomped on it in the straightaway. Coogle, still ahead of him, was creeping up steadily, trying to wedge his way between the two cars in front of him. Bart kept on his tail.

Giving him a draft? Possibly. At this point Jim wasn't hooked into the radio chatter between the driver and his spotter, who was even higher up than they were, watching the race from a more objective vantage point.

In what had become a reflex action, Jim plugged in the earpiece dangling from the small scanner clipped to his belt. The device, essentially a CB radio in "listen only" mode, was already tuned in to the team's frequency.

"Ask Volmer for a draft," he heard Bart instruct his spotter.

The draft was an effective tactic for getting ahead of the competition, but it left the man in the lead vulnerable to the very person who helped him. Two or more cars would form a chain, the second car hugging the bumper of the first. Together they would be able to reach higher speeds than singly, but the close proximity of the trailing car disabled the function of the spoiler on the trunk of the lead car. Instead of it pushing down the rear end and giving him greater road traction, it allowed the rear end to float, and left him highly susceptible to centrifugal force in turns. A bump would completely destabilize him.

A moment after Bart's call, the No. 468 car was tight on his tail. They approached Turn One.

"Offer Coogle a draft," Bart now directed.

The snake line of three cars slithered around Turns One and Two, passing two cars on the inside. The trio naturally migrated to midtrack coming out of the second turn. Three car lengths separated Coogle in the lead from the pack in front of him.

"Tell Volmer to stay with me," Bart told his spotter.

"Roger that."

Before Coogle had a chance to veer back to the left, Bart slingshotted to the inside of the track. With Volmer stuck on his tail, giving him the extra boost of speed he needed, they both zipped passed Coogle.

"Sweet move," Jim murmured. A quick glance to his right, however, suggested Jessup didn't share his exhilaration, though he said nothing to explain why.

Bart and Volmer made another circuit, then broke off as the traffic around them thickened. Bart was moving up on Jem Nordstrom when Coogle appeared in his rearview mirror. The spotter said he was offering a draft.

"Good."

Already the rookie was hugging Bart's tailpipe.

Then came the tap.

Was it intentional...or a miscalculation? In such close quarters and from his angle of observation Jim couldn't tell. Didn't matter.

Destabilized, Bart began the inexorable drift to the right, as white smoke funneled from his rear tires which had lost their traction and were spinning on the coarse pavement.

Jim knew that for the moment at least his driver was out of control.

Coogle tried to replicate Bart's earlier slingshot tactic by moving up into the space Bart had vacated on the left, but he had miscalculated, found himself boxed in and forced to slow down.

They were at Turn Three now. Bart, able to maintain his car's forward orientation but still unable to reestablish traction under power, struck the wall, bounced off it and ricocheted back into the flow of traffic.

The first car he hit was Coogle's. In the blink of an eye,

Coogle slammed into No. 426, which was advancing on his right. Bart struck Coogle again and was then hit by No. 437, which had been directly behind him. Car No. 426, which was now on the inside, miraculously escaped, as did No. 437, though they were far behind the lead pack at this point.

Bart was billowing blue-gray smoke as he skidded helplessly onto the infield, his right front tire canted at an unnatural angle. Coogle, still behind him, nosedived into the grass a dozen yards away, flipped once, rolled, and came to rest rightside up, his radiator emitting a wispy cloud of white steam.

The yellow caution flag fluttered angrily. The word went out on radios. Track speeds declined.

"So much for catching up on points in this race," Mark Jessup sneered.

No disputing that. It was remotely possible that they'd be able to get the car back on the track to finish the race—merely finishing garnered some points—but it was highly doubtful.

TWENTY MINUTES LATER, JIM was in the garage area. Car No. 475 had been towed off the track and was being examined by the engineering team, not that there was anything they could do about the wreck at this point. For this race Bart Branch was a DNF—did not finish—again. How much of the car could be salvaged was still an open question. It appeared to be a total wreck, but appearances could be deceiving. Replacing crumpled bodywork was routine, as long as the chassis was still in alignment. The engineers back in Charlotte would evaluate the structure very carefully to determine if it was.

Jim moved over to the side where Phil was conferring with Gary Wells, his chief engineer.

"Did Bart slow down just before Coogle hit him?" Jim asked Phil after Gary excused himself to rejoin the team.

"My guess is that he'll say no, and Coogle will say yes," the team chief responded.

"You think it was revenge for Bart getting around him earlier?"

Phil shrugged, though it was clear that was exactly what he thought. "No way of proving it one way or the other. One man's word against another's."

"The end result is the same," Jim noted. Another car wrecked. The blame game wouldn't do anyone any good.

"It might have been different," Anita said, "if Coogle had been less impulsive. Temper on a track can be dangerous."

Jim hadn't even seen her come in, a good indication of how preoccupied he was with the entire situation. Lately he seemed to have developed radar where she was concerned.

"Coogle's a rookie," Jim reminded her. "It'd be different if one of the old heads like Dean Grosso was in that car. Bart should have remembered that."

"Is he still at the care center?" Anita asked Phil.

"I just got word. They've already released him. He should be here in a couple of minutes."

"I'd like the three of us to meet later and talk this through," Jim told Phil. "Things are going to have to change." He didn't mention that Jessup had threatened to drop EZ-Plus's sponsorship unless things improved, even if it meant paying a penalty.

Anita nodded. "I don't recommend you do it today. Get a night's sleep first. Give everyone time to calm down."

Bart climbed out of the back of a small white pickup and approached the three people.

"You okay?" Jim asked, genuinely concerned in spite of his disappointment.

"I'm fine," he said, his voice rising, "but if I ever get my hands on that—" he looked at Anita and stifled his words. Jim doubted she would have been shocked by them, but he appreciated Bart's showing her deference.

Another truck passed them and stopped at a garage bay two spaces down. Turning on his heel, fists clenched, Bart approached the man in the driving uniform who opened the passenger door.

The scream of race cars still on the track made it impossible to hear the exchange between the two drivers, but it wasn't necessary; their body language said it all. There was no mistaking what happened next. Coogle raised his fist and swung it directly at Bart's face.

Fortunately Bart was fast enough to turn his head so that the knuckles missed his nose. Instead the impact of Coogle's fist caught him in the orbit just above his left eye. Instinct took over and Bart did a roundhouse to Coogle's midsection. Coogle averted that blow, but not before landing an uppercut to his opponent's jaw.

By then, Jim and Phil had rushed forward. Jim grabbed Bart from behind, pinning his arms at his sides in an iron grip and momentarily lifting him off the ground, while Phil planted himself with outstretched arms between the two adversaries. Meantime, a couple of Coogle's teammates, standing nearby, had sprung into action and were jointly holding back their man.

"Cool it," Jim whispered right up against Bart's ear. It wasn't friendly advice; it was an order. "Now."

Bart was like spring steel, ready to snap. Jim, an inch

taller and carrying at least twenty pounds more of muscle, tightened his lock hold around the man's waist.

"Now," Jim repeated sternly.

Endless seconds elapsed before the infuriated driver was able to get his emotions sufficiently under control for Jim to relax his grip. Still, he held onto Bart for several more seconds before actually releasing him. As he did so, he saw a racing fan, with a garage pass dangling from a lanyard around his neck, aiming a small camcorder. Great!

The whole incident had been caught on tape. Jim managed to hold back the word that instantly sprang up.

"The hauler," Jim barked to his driver. "Don't stop or talk to anyone. Just go directly there."

Jim and Phil spent the next ten minutes trying to calm people down. Clyde Coogle's teammates were ready to rumble. To Jim's surprise it was Clyde, the instigator of the violence who became a cool head and called off the dogs. When he and his people had finally returned to their bay, Jim looked about, expecting to see Anita, but she was nowhere in sight.

"Went after the guy with the camcorder," Harv Kristol, one of the tire changers, told him.

Jim should have realized she'd be looking at the public-relations impact. For that he was grateful to her. Contrary to folk wisdom, not all publicity was good.

He invited Phil to join him and together they entered the hauler and walked up to the lounge in the front. Bart was there, a sports drink in his hand, looking like a defiant teenager. Jim got himself a bottle of water from the small refrigerator.

There were so many things he could say. That he was disappointed in Bart. That he wanted an explanation for his performance on the track, for this third crash this season, and for his even more stupid actions in the garage area. That he could have sympathized with him having a bad day, commiserated on how things seemed to be ganging up on him. But none of those observations would have done any good.

"I'm putting you on notice, Branch. Another episode like we just witnessed a few minutes ago and you're off the team. You're not likely to make the cut for the Chase after being eliminated today. Catching up and getting into the top ten is a near impossibility now, so dropping you from the team won't be a problem. Someone else can drive the No. 475 car for the remainder of the season."

Branch steamed but wisely said nothing, and Jim had to give the guy grudging respect for that, at least.

"Our next concern is NASCAR. Your invading Coogle's garage area and the fight that followed got taped, so there won't be any way to deny what happened, much less hide it. The pictures will speak for themselves. NASCAR will probably suspend you, in which case your competing for the rest of the season will be a moot point anyway."

Still the driver, the more laid back of the twins, said nothing. That didn't fool Jim. He knew the man wasn't being blasé. In fact, he suspected it was taking a supreme effort of will for him to keep from exploding. Jim had to give him points for that, too, and rather than tempt fate any more, he left the hauler.

Outside, the air reeked of the smells that made NASCAR unique. Fuel and lubricant, burned rubber and hot asphalt, the acrid stench of ozone from fried electrical wires. Jim pressed a speed-dial button on his cell phone. It was picked up halfway through the second ring.

"Where are you?" he asked.

"In the NASCAR office," Anita replied, sounding distracted, "hoping to get in to see one of the officials and maybe mitigate some of the impact of this. I want to point out that Bart didn't start the fight. He didn't throw the first punch. He was just defending himself, like any real man would…and should."

Jim almost laughed at having his own words tossed back in his face…er…ear. If the situation weren't so serious, he would have.

"Did you recover the tape?" he asked.

"No. I tried to catch up with the guy but he'd already hightailed it. Someone said they thought they'd seen him leaving the infield with a network reporter."

"Crap."

"I made a similar comment. Different word, though."

This time Jim did chuckle, and he wondered at this gorgeous redhead who was able to take the sting out of the most disappointing situations. "Keep me posted."

"Yes, sir." She hung up.

CHAPTER TWENTY-ONE

WHEN HE GOT TO THE AIRPORT that evening, Jim discovered Gideon Taney pacing in the private airplane passenger terminal. Jim greeted him and asked if there was some sort of air-traffic delay.

"Fuel pump problem. My mechanics think it may only be a fuse and can have it resolved in a matter of minutes."

"Where are you headed?"

"Charlotte. I have a meeting with a corporate sponsor there first thing in the morning."

"That's where I'm going. Why don't you have your people transfer your baggage to my plane, and you come with me? That'll give your crew whatever time they need to check things out."

"You don't mind?"

"Not at all. My son's opted to drive home with some of his friends—" Kylie and her son "—so I'm on my own. Be grateful for the company."

"I appreciate this, Jim. My next option was to see if I could wrangle a commercial flight tonight, but I've been told everything's booked solid, so it would have to be on standby."

Twenty minutes later they were taxiing down the runway.

"Quite a dustup your driver had today in the garage area," Taney remarked with a chuckle after they had taken off and the steward had served them drinks.

Uncomfortable about the whole incident, Jim tried to make light of it with a flip comment about drivers being willing to do just about anything to get attention.

Taney smiled and took an appreciative sip of his single-malt Scotch. "Have you thought about my offer?"

"It's still too early for me to make a decision of that sort, and until Uncle Richard's condition stabilizes, I don't really feel free to pursue it."

"But you *are* interested." A statement as much as a question.

"Oh, it's something to consider, in theory at least," Jim acknowledged. There didn't seem to be much point in trying to deny it. "The thing is," he added, "I don't have enough data on which to base a decision."

The other man nodded, the hint of a smirk on his lips. "I hear you." He swirled the amber liquid in his glass for a moment. "Okay, toy with the number thirty-five."

Jim nearly gasped. Was the man offering thirty-five million dollars for PDQ? It certainly sounded that way. His own calculations had put the value of the team fairly close to that amount, slightly lower, actually, but he'd expected an initial offer to be considerably below that. Did this mean he'd miscalculated? That the team was actually worth significantly more? Made him wonder what he might have missed.

"It's a generous offer, Jim," Taney said. "I think you know that."

"Yes, it is, and I'm asking myself why you're starting out so high."

Taney laughed. "We can quibble if you want to, but I

think you get my point. I want your team, and I'm willing to pay a fair, even generous, price for it."

The man was frank. Jim liked that.

Taney took another swig from his glass and studied the remaining contents intently.

"We're very different personalities, you and I," he said. "You like things to be quiet and predictable. I, on the other hand, thrive on controversy. There's a good deal of controversy inherent in the PDQ team. You see it as a detriment. I see it as an advantage, a welcome challenge. With the Branch brothers there's plenty to keep the public interested, buzzing—the competition between twins, their father's notoriety. You mentioned that some drivers will do anything to get attention. The fact is, I enjoy stirring the pot. It's helped make me rich, and it's lined the pockets of my team members, as well."

They talked some more, eventually straying into subjects that had nothing to do with NASCAR. Jim found himself in the strange position of liking the man and enjoying his company, while being distinctly unlike him in approach and tactics. Jim had never considered himself an introvert or particularly conservative in temperament, but compared with Gideon Taney he was. Yet Taney didn't wear loud plaid sports jackets like Uncle Richard often did, and he wasn't a back slapper.

They parted on amiable terms at the airport in Charlotte where Taney's limo was waiting for him at the terminal. Jim got into his SUV and drove back to his uncle's house.

He sat at the desk in the den late that night, the day's race silently animating the large wall screen, and doodled on a pad. He kept replaying his discussion with Gideon Taney. He had one more question to ask him, but it could wait.

ON MONDAY AFTERNOON, by prearrangement, Jim and Anita met in Richard's room in the medical complex's rehabilitation centre. Jim had already spoken with his uncle's doctor and received the latest update on his condition. Richard's speech was improving, though he still had noticeable facial paralysis on the right side. He was experiencing tingling in his right arm, which, while annoying, was deemed a good sign. It meant his body hadn't given up trying to mend itself. Richard was receiving medication to alleviate some of the discomfort. After six weeks, he still had little sensation in his right leg, however.

"Be honest with me, doc. What's the long-term prognosis?"

Leaning back in a squeaky swivel chair, the physician steepled his fingers a moment before answering. "We can probably look forward to further progress in the areas of speech and manual function, but I seriously doubt touch typing or ballroom dancing is in his future. In fact, the chances of his ever walking again seem extremely remote."

This only confirmed what Jim already suspected.

"If he were a younger man with greater energy reserves, his potential would be better. I'm not ruling out the possibility of improvement in mobility, but I don't think it's something we should count on. At this point, therapy will have to focus on learning to adjust to his disabilities rather than overcoming them. I'm sorry."

"I appreciate your candor, Doctor. How much of this does my uncle know?"

"The therapists and I have emphasized the positive with him, explaining what improvements are possible. But your uncle is an intelligent man. I think he understands, without anyone spelling it out, that his prospects for significant future improvement aren't great. I don't recommend holding out false or unrealistic hope, but a good deal of his ability to cope with his situation is a matter of mental attitude."

"Saw race," Richard said now. He was stammering less, and while enunciating some sounds was still a strain, he had learned to use a minimum number of words to convey his thoughts. "Enjoyed."

"Until the fight," Jim remarked, unable to disguise his annoyance.

"Exciting."

"It was that," Anita agreed cheerfully. "They're going to be playing that thirty seconds episode for a long, long time."

Along with video of the crash itself, sportscasts had been featuring it. She seemed to be pleased at the prospect, whereas in Jim's mind it was something to be downplayed, since the move had been such a dumb one.

"Lucky tourist," Richard said. "Picture."

"For him," Jim countered glumly. "Not for us."

Richard smiled at Anita. "Does not understand."

"What don't I understand?" Recalling Taney's summary of the differences between them, Jim felt as if the joke was on him.

"Fight," his uncle explained. "Natural. Old days more. Fun for fans."

Jim thought back to some of the classic rivalries. They didn't always result in fisticuffs, but a few of them had, and the ones that had been captured on film were favorite clips that were included in nearly every documentary. Thirty, forty and fifty years after the events, people still smiled when they saw them. Maybe Jim needed to take a longer view of this incident, as well.

"If NASCAR officials suspend him for even one race, when they meet tomorrow, it'll destroy any chance Bart might have had of making the Chase, never mind winning the Cup."

"Won't," Richard said. "Only fine."

So he thought Bart would be fined but not suspended.

"I wouldn't be so sure," Jim commented. "In the past few years they've come down pretty hard on fighting."

"He didn't throw the first punch," Anita reminded him yet again. Her eyes twinkled. "Surely swinging back in self-defense is acceptable."

Jim knew she was taunting him. He could hardly blame her. In fact he'd come to enjoy their jibes at each other, like inside jokes they alone understood. He just hoped in this case she was right.

They talked more about the race, about Bart's overall performance. Jim was a bit taken aback by his uncle's attitude. Richard was convinced the twin was a good driver, and though this wasn't turning out to be an especially good year for him, the old man was confident Bart had enormous potential in the NASCAR Sprint Cup Series in the future and should be given every break.

Jim had tremendous respect for his uncle's instincts, but he wondered if this time, the old timer might be wrong in his evaluation. It left Jim with an unbalanced feeling he didn't like. He was used to making decisions based on facts and figures, not wishful thinking or gut feelings. He just wasn't built that way.

Maybe it was time he more aggressively explored the sell option.

As she had the past few weeks, Anita came over to Richard's house Monday afternoon, bringing her bikini with her, along with toiletries, in a small canvas tote.

She was sitting on a chaise longue beside the pool, applying sunscreen to her arms, when Jim joined her. He'd met her at the front door fully clothed, but now, coming out onto the patio through the kitchen, he was wearing only a swimsuit and sandals. The sight of him was magnetic, and she had to fight the constant battle between staring at his powerfully built body and trying to ignore it. No contest. The eyes won every time.

He stood over her. "May I help?" She heard the eagerness in his voice and shared it. When she didn't immediately respond, he said, "Lie down on your stomach, and I'll get your back."

First she took another sip of her iced tea and wondered if she needed something stronger to cure the tingling in her belly, though to be honest she wasn't sure she wanted it to go away. After all, there was tingling, and there was tingling.

Jim nudged her hip with his and settled at her side, then began applying sunscreen to her shoulders and back, and giving her a soothing massage in the process. Well, maybe soothing was the wrong word. The power of his strong hands, firm but gentle, was relaxing and stimulating at the same time.

"It's sort of quiet around here without Billy," she mumbled out of the side of her mouth.

"Kylie called here right after noon today," Jim explained, "to say they'd arrived home safely and that Ryan and a couple of his buddies were camping out tonight in the backyard. She wanted to know if Billy could stay and join them."

"I bet that was a tough decision," she mumbled, her cheek against the soft bath sheet she'd spread across the chaise cushion. "Oh, oh, right there, yeah."

Jim dug his knuckles just a bit more vigorously into her shoulder muscles. "Almost seven-eighths of a second by my reckoning," he said. "I reminded him it was Monday and that you always come for dinner on Monday nights, but he said you'd be here next Monday, too, and he could see you then. Besides, he just saw you yesterday, and I would be here to eat dinner with you—"

Her groan of pleasure rippled into slurred words. "I suppose I should be offended."

"I'll ground him," Jim said as he moved his hands down and planted a kiss at the nape of her neck.

She skewed her head and opened her right eye long enough to look up at him to see if he was serious. He wasn't, of course, and it amazed her that she still had trouble gauging him sometimes. She breathed in and out slowly as he applied cool sunscreen onto her warm skin and rubbed it in.

"What are you planning to burn for dinner tonight?" she asked.

He snorted. "I should never have told you about the burgers. Red snapper," he said, "and it won't be burned, it'll be blackened, with roasted corn on the cob and a wilted spinach salad."

"Mmm." She'd discovered over the past weeks that he was actually a very good cook, especially on the grill. "Sounds delicious." At the moment, the menu barely registered. All she could think of were the delicious sensations rippling through her as he worked his hands on her body and her growing awareness of his hip pressed against her thigh.

"Key lime pie for dessert," he added.

"If you ever get tired of number crunching you can always open a restaurant. That'd give you plenty of stuff to count. Including receipts."

He chuckled, but she could sense in the shyness of his laugh that he was pleased by the compliment.

"You're going to spoil me," she said a minute later.

"Now, there's an idea."

He applied the cream to the back of her left leg and spread it out in long sweeping motions with both hands, then repeated the process on the other leg. As his hands moved from calf to lower thigh to upper thigh, heat built within her and her pulse picked up extra beats.

"But it would be with an ulterior motive," he murmured in her ear.

He was so close, she could feel the heat radiating off his broad, bare chest. She flipped over onto her back. "Whatever could it possibly be?"

He bent and kissed her lightly on the lips. "It would all be a ruse, a subterfuge, you see." He touched his lips to hers again. "A cunning device for getting you into my bed."

She batted her lashes dramatically. "I'm very flattered, Jim, but you really don't have to go to all that trouble."

The corners of his eyes crinkled. "Yeah, I do," he assured her in the most serious of tones. "Because I'll have to eat if I'm going to get all the nourishment I'll need to keep up my strength when I finally succeed in my quest."

"Your strength." The laugh that erupted arose from deep inside her. "Now that sounds like a challenge."

"Oh, it is." He clasped her hands in his, rose to his feet and pulled her up with him, then extended his arms around her waist. Nuzzling her neck, he muttered, "You make me hot, Anita."

The feel of his naked chest against her skin was scorching, unbalancing.

Suddenly they were tumbling into the pool. She surfaced—sputtering—only to find herself still encircled by his arms. She reached up to pull the hair off her face.

"You're wet," he said, grinning.

And at this moment as happy as I've ever been, she wanted to tell him. "I wonder why."

His hold on her had been loose, but now he tightened it. The water around them may have been cool, but his flesh wasn't. Neither was hers.

He brought his mouth down to her. The taste of his kiss was familiar, yet a new adventure, one she wanted to explore for a very long time.

"Wait," she said, breaking off. "Dinner. You promised me food."

He snickered and rubbed his nose against hers. "I changed my mind."

She gazed at him, feeling bubbly inside, not sure what he was referring to, not sure she could reverse course, no matter what decision he had made.

"No fish tonight," he said. "I need red meat. Plenty of it."

She grinned. "Don't forget the oysters."

He kissed her again.

"Hadn't we better get started then?" she asked, as if they hadn't already.

"Oh, it started some time ago." He nuzzled her neck. They were definitely on the same wavelength here. "It began that first day, when you bumped into me."

"You mean when you snuck up and crowded me," she corrected him, "and practically knocked me off my feet." Then she added, "Actually, you did knock me off my feet. I just didn't know it at the time."

His fingers roamed her sides, stroked the outside of her thighs, lifted her legs so they fit naturally around his hips.

"In fact," she said, "you still have me floating off my feet."

He kissed her again. "I'll do my best to keep you there."

FIRST, THEY ATE DINNER, keeping to the original menu of spicy snapper and crunchy sweet corn. They dined outside and washed it all down with a crisp, dry white wine. All the while the air around them crackled with sexual tension and anticipation.

The sun set. They sat in parallel chaise longues, held hands and talked, though Anita doubted either of them could have remembered what they discussed. Nothing. Everything. The words didn't matter. What was important was that they were together, sharing each other's company. In tune. In synch. *In love?*

She felt as if she were suspended in a make-believe world where there were no cares, no worries, no other people. In those precious moments, there were just the two of them—Jim and Anita, man and woman. Lover and beloved. Each both.

They went into the pool again, though neither of them made an effort to swim. They stood where the water was deep enough to come up to her shoulders, his chest.

When he kissed her this time her pulse raced, and she wondered why the water around her didn't boil up. Yearnings, cravings, selfish demands took possession of her. Fiendish needs left her defenseless, short of breath, heart pounding. She pressed herself to him, savored the masculine firmness she found and clutched him all the harder.

"You said something about taking me to your bed," she whispered in his ear, though there was certainly no one around to hear. "I think it's time to keep your promise."

CHAPTER TWENTY-TWO

HE HAD FALLEN ASLEEP, curled against Anita's soft, warm body, when the phone rang. He jolted awake, and in doing so woke her. She murmured sounds he didn't quite understand as he pried his eyes open enough to see the digital clock on the bedside table. A few minutes past one. There was no readout on this telephone; he picked up the receiver and muttered hello.

"Jim, I'm sorry if I woke you."

He was tempted to say she did, and had to bite back the impulse to ask who the hell was calling. The voice was familiar, if he could only get his head clear. "Not a problem," he said, hoping his enunciation no longer betrayed his sleepiness. "Who—"

"It's Kylie, Jim."

The fog instantly lifted. Kylie Palmer. Billy was spending the night camping in her backyard with her son, Ryan, and some other kids.

He propped himself up on one elbow. "What's wrong? Is Billy all right?"

"He's fine…or mostly fine. It's the other kid who isn't."

A knot of dread formed in the pit of Jim's stomach. "What's happened?"

"Billy got into another fight, this time with Mitchell Dugway."

Jim bolted completely upright. "Got into a fight?" he repeated. "Is anyone hurt? Need medical attention?"

"Nothing that serious, but Mitch's dad is coming over to pick him up. I thought you might want to be here when—"

"I'm on my way." Jim hung up the phone.

"Who was that?" Anita asked, as she pulled herself into a sitting position against the bed's headboard, instinctively drawing the sheet up in front of her.

"Kylie." He was already on his feet and moving buck-naked toward the bathroom. "Billy's been in another fight."

"Uh-oh."

Jim jumped into the shower, to wake himself up completely. Two minutes later, he stepped out and found Anita putting down a toothbrush she'd apparently found in a drawer. The wrapper was lying on the marble counter.

"Go back to bed," he said, reaching for a towel. "No sense in both of us losing sleep."

"I'm coming with you. I wouldn't be able to sleep now, anyway. I'd be too busy worrying about you and Billy."

He stopped drying himself long enough to kiss her softly on the lips. "I'm not sure that's a good idea, sweetheart." He draped the towel across his shoulders, tugged it back and forth, saw her eyes watching him and knew he'd better get dressed quickly. "How do we explain your being with me at this hour of the night?"

"I don't think we'll scandalize Kylie or the father of the boy Billie fought with."

She reached behind her and rotated the shower control to adjust the water temperature.

"I was thinking about Billy," he said.

Of course he was. His son was his first priority, and she

admired him for it. "I doubt he's focused on the time right now. All he's thinking about is that he's in trouble. He knew I was coming here this evening. Why don't we just say I hadn't left yet when Ryan's mom called? It's true, after all."

He snorted, pleased at her wanting to be by his side, and agreed they didn't owe anyone an explanation. That didn't prevent people from asking questions, however, and drawing judgments, whether they received answers or not.

A mischievous smile crept across her face. "I suggest you put some clothes on, if you expect us to ever get out of here."

"Wise, as well as beautiful," he said. "I'm sorry to spoil your evening like this."

She raised herself up on tiptoe and, being careful not to make any other body contact, kissed him on the cheek. "Nothing for you to apologize for. I assure you." Still grinning, she patted his cheek which was coarse with yesterday's whiskers. "Nothing at all."

He was tucking his short-sleeve plaid shirt into his jeans by the time she emerged from the steamy bathroom a couple of minutes later, and again he couldn't keep his eyes from traveling the length of her smooth feminine body. "I'll make this up to you."

"I'll hold you to that," she said as she began quickly putting on yesterday's clothes.

He let out an audible sigh. "You sure you want to come with me? You don't have to. You can wait here for us, or at home. I'll call you."

"Not a chance."

They set the security alarm and left her car in the driveway. They took his car over to Kylie Palmer's house, which was only about a mile away.

"Did she give you any details about what happened?" Anita asked, as they rolled through deserted streets.

"Only that he'd gotten into a fight with one of the other kids and the kid's father was on his way over to pick him up."

"I'm sure there's a perfectly reasonable explanation."

"I hope so or Billy is going to find himself grounded for life, or at least until he's thirty-seven."

She chuckled. Humor at this stage was a good sign.

"Don't be too hard on him. He's just a kid trying to make sense of a world that sometimes doesn't make a whole lot of sense."

"Yeah, I know." He turned onto the street where the Palmers lived. "Thank you for tonight."

She reached over and placed her hand over his on the steering wheel. "The feeling is mutual, believe me."

A minute later he pulled up the Palmer driveway. The two-story brick-and-stone house was lit up and looked strangely welcoming in the warm summer night.

He shut off the engine, got out and started around to Anita's door, but she already had it open and was climbing out. Taking her hand, they walked together up the concrete path to the front door. It wasn't until they were halfway there that he realized how natural it felt to have her hand in his.

He rang the bell.

Kylie opened the door, looking momentarily stunned to see Anita with him, but quickly hid her surprise. "Hi," she said to both of them. "We're in the kitchen. Mitch's father, Lyle, isn't here yet, but he should be any moment."

"What happened?"

She closed the door and led them over to the side rather than out to the kitchen.

"After the boys finally quieted down around midnight, Mitch apparently decided to play a practical joke on Billy. The two had been taunting each other all evening. After Billy dozed off, Mitch tied a rope around Billy's ankle, then jostled him and shouted fire." She shook her head. "It's one of the oldest tricks in the book, but every generation thinks it's just invented it. Anyway, Billy jumped up, fell flat on his face and pulled the tent down on top of him. Didn't hurt anybody, but naturally Billy got mad. Mitch made it worse by laughing and teasing him for being so clumsy. Billy untied the rope, walked over and socked him."

Jim shook his head. "Bad?"

"Not the first time. Apparently it was as much a shove as a punch. Mitch made some comment about him hitting like a girl. That's when Billy let him have it."

Jim looked at her questioningly.

"Mitch has a pretty good-size bruise on his cheek. Probably have a shiner tomorrow, as well as a fat lip. Not a drop of blood was shed, though, as far as I can tell."

"No serious damage done, then?"

"Not really, Jim."

"Who told you all this?" Anita asked.

"Got most of it from Nick. He was the fourth one in their tent, and Ryan has backed him up."

"What's Mitch's story?"

Kylie rolled her eyes. "That he was the innocent victim of premeditated aggression, of course. Mr. Innocence insists he didn't do anything, that Billy just got tangled up in some rope they were using to practice making knots with and tripped. Insists he had nothing to do with tying his feet."

"And Billy? What does he say?" Anita pressed.

"Not much. He hasn't disputed what Nick and Ryan have said."

"You know these kids better than I do, Kylie," Jim said. "Who do you believe?"

"I shouldn't have agreed to let Ryan invite Mitch over in the first place," Kylie said without hesitation. "He's pulled stunts like this before. So you can blame it partially on me."

Jim shook his head, and they started moving toward the kitchen, when the doorbell rang.

"That'll be his father."

Jim remained where he was, while Kylie crossed the room, checked the peephole and opened the door.

"I got here as soon as I could." A big-boned man walked through the doorway. He was several inches over six feet and weighed enough that, if he were a football player, he'd probably be called the meat locker or something similar. "Where is he? Is he all right?"

"He's fine," Kylie assured him as she closed the door. While he stood there, waiting for her, he eyed Jim.

"Lyle Dugway, this is Jim Latimer," Kylie said.

Jim took the initiative to go over to him, his hand outstretched. "Sorry we have to meet under these circumstances."

Dugway accepted it but only briefly. "What happened?"

"Sounds like an overreaction to a practical joke," Jim said. "I was just about to get the details myself."

Dugway was the kind of colossus who dominated a room by his sheer presence. He could have been a gentle giant, but that wasn't the impression Jim received, more the type who took advantage of the intimidation inherent in his size.

"Let's go talk to the boys," Kylie offered.

Dugway followed immediately behind her, letting Jim and Anita catch up. He'd never asked her name or her reason for being there. A non-entity. Not a positive sign in Jim's estimation. He had never met the man's son, but he realized the father didn't leave him sympathetically disposed toward the boy. But of course that wasn't being fair. A son was not responsible for his father. By now that lesson should have been learned.

The four boys were sitting around the kitchen table, glasses of milk before them. Mitchell had finished his and Nick had drunk about half of his, while the other two boys had barely touched theirs.

Billy looked up at his father, suddenly contrite. He knew he was in trouble and made no attempt to offer a preemptive defense. Then he saw Anita. "You came, too," he mumbled, his eyes brightening for a fleeting minute.

Lyle examined his son, turning the kid's head this way and that. "You okay?"

"Yeah," the boy replied in that peculiar tone that was both a whine and a brave front, the blameless victim of injustice.

He had his father's features as well as his large bone structure. Because of the company he was in, Jim assumed he was the same age as the other boys, between ten or twelve, but he could have passed for a teenager in size. A purplish-red bruise blossomed on his left cheekbone; his upper lip was swollen.

"What happened?" his father asked peevishly.

"I was sleeping." Mitch's speech was slurred by his distorted mouth. "This stupid kid grabs me by the shirt and punches me in the face. Twice. I was only half awake and didn't have a chance to fight back. The other guys had to yank him off me."

Jim caught the expression on Kylie's face. She tipped a brow just enough to indicate she didn't buy this version of events, either. Billy had temper problems from time to time and occasionally overreacting, but this kind of unprovoked aggression was completely out of character.

"He tied my leg to the tent post, then yelled and woke me up," Billy countered. "When I jumped, the tent fell down."

"He got his leg caught in a rope we were using," Mitch charged. "I didn't tie him."

"Yes, you did," Nick shouted. "I saw you."

"Is that the way you saw it, too?" Jim asked Ryan.

Ryan looked over at his mother who nodded for him to answer.

"Mitch tied Billy's foot to one of the tent stakes," he said, "then shouted for him to run quick 'cause the tent was on fire. Billy bolted and went crashing, and pulled down the tent with him."

Jim addressed his son. "Did you hit Mitch?"

Billy's lips began to quiver. He controlled them. "Yes, sir."

"Did he hit you first?"

"He tripped me."

"That's not what I asked. Did he hit you first?"

"I guess not, but doesn't him tying my leg—"

"Apologize to Mitch."

"He—" Billy started, saw the determined expression on his father's face, lowered his head and mumbled, "I'm sorry."

"Not good enough. Raise your head, look at Mitch and tell him you're sorry you hit him."

"I'm not sorry I hit him," Billy shouted back. "He tied my leg to the tent first. You're not being fair." He started to narrow his eyes and glare at his father, but lost his nerve and looked down.

Jim was stunned. Billy had been rebellious before, but he had never defied his father, never challenged him in front of someone else. As he studied his son he realized he wasn't completely sure how he felt about the situation. For the moment they'd reached an impasse, one that wasn't about to go away soon or easily. The room remained silent for what must have seemed like an eternity to the boy.

Finally Jim turned to Lyle Dugway. "Take your son home, Mr. Dugway. You don't have to worry about any more incidents of this nature."

"Your kid has a problem, Latimer. You need to get him help."

Jim was tempted to tell him his son had the bigger problem, but didn't imagine a war of words would improve the situation.

It took a couple of minutes for Mitchell to get his things and precede his father to the luxury sedan parked at the curb. During it all, no one said a word. No thank-yous were offered by father or son to Kylie for her hospitality.

"Good riddance," she mumbled, as the car pulled away.

"Get your things, too," Jim instructed his son when they returned to the kitchen.

"Do I have to? Why can't I stay?"

"Do as you're told, and get your things."

Hang dog, Billy followed orders.

CHAPTER TWENTY-THREE

ANITA CHOSE TO SIT in the backseat with Billy while Jim drove home to Richard's house. He listened intently to their conversation. No recriminations on her part, no lectures, though Jim knew her attitude about fighting. Billy's answers were concise and guarded at first, but the more they talked, the more they lowered their voices, and the warmer their conversation seemed to become, to the point that Jim was beginning to get just a little bit jealous of being excluded.

He turned down the driveway to Richard's mansion, hit the button over the visor to remotely open the garage door and turn off the alarm system. He pulled into the middle bay, between Richard's two cars.

"Billy, go to your room, get dressed for bed, then come back downstairs," Jim ordered before anyone had a chance to open their car doors. "We're not finished yet."

Billy dragged his knapsack with him and entered the house.

JIM AND ANITA CLIMBED OUT of the SUV. Behind it, he reached for her hand. In the shadows beyond the glare of the security lights, he kissed her briefly and softly on the lips.

"No need for you to hang around," he told her. "I'll call you tomorrow."

"I'd like to stay, if you don't mind. Just for a few minutes," she added, lest he think she was suggesting they share his bed again, something she would very much like to do. Especially now. With so much tension between them, she felt desperate to touch and be touched.

"It's not necessary," he assured her, but she could see his desire for company was as strong as hers, even if they couldn't satisfy it the way they both wanted to, not with Billy in the house.

They entered by the kitchen door.

"I'm going to have orange juice," Jim said. "Want some?"

She hadn't realized she was thirsty. "Thanks."

He poured them each small glasses. They were taking them into the living room when Billy descended the stairs and came into the room, wearing baggy gym shorts and a white T-shirt, not moving in his usual bouncy fashion, but solemnly.

Jim sat in the high-back upholstered chair by the writing table.

"Tell me again what happened tonight," he instructed the boy.

Billy stood in front of him and recounted the events that had brought him there.

The four boys had been roughhousing in the tent, he said. Mitch Dugway was big, but he wasn't very well-coordinated or fast, and Billy had been able to get him in several lock positions. He was getting really mad when Ryan said they had to stop it before his mom came out and yelled at them to go to sleep. Mitch wanted to keep going, but Ryan convinced him to settle down.

"I fell asleep a few minutes later. The next thing I knew, Mitch was yelling something about fire and that we had to get out of the tent quick. I jumped up, took one step and fell flat on my face, bringing the tent down on top of me."

"Where were the other boys?" Anita asked, mindful even before she posed the question that it wasn't her place to interfere, but she thought she knew the answer, and in her estimation, it made a difference.

"They were already outside," he said.

"What happened then?" Jim asked.

"Mitch started laughing at me, but the others didn't. That's when I saw the rope tied around my ankle and knew I'd been tricked. So I untied it, got up, went over to Mitch and swung at him. He ducked, then laughed harder. So, I really let him have it," Billy concluded, unaware that it sounded like a brag.

"He was playing a practical joke on you," Jim stated.

Billy looked as if he wanted to argue the point, but there really wasn't much he could say, so he only nodded.

"And because you couldn't take the joke, you hit him."

"He started it, Dad."

"Started what? He didn't hit you."

"But—"

"I've told you about starting fights before, haven't I? You understand the difference between playing games and hitting someone to hurt them, don't you?"

Billy lowered his head and mumbled, "Yes, sir."

"Since you refuse to obey the rules, I'm suspending your attendance at driving school."

Billy's eyes went wide, then began to tear up. "But, Dad, that's not fair. He started it."

"He tricked you, and maybe he was being mean. That still didn't give you the right to punch him."

Tears of frustration and anger were spilling down the boy's cheeks, and Anita thought her heart would break. But Jim was right.

"That's all, Billy. You can go up to bed now."

In a mad retreat the boy ran up the stairs, tripped and fell forward on one of the steps, but kept going. A second later his door closed a bit more forcefully than usual, but not quite hard enough to fully qualify as a slam.

Anita got up from the couch. "I know you're right, Jim, but that punishment is pretty harsh, isn't it?"

He rose as well. "Punishment that doesn't exact a price isn't punishment. Billy knows the rules, and he disobeyed them. Actions have consequences, Anita. As I recall, you abhor violence, even in response to violence."

"I do."

"He's not a little boy. All too soon he's going to be a man, but he won't be much of a man if he doesn't learn now to control his temper and to be judicious in his use of force."

"How long will you withhold driving school from him?"

"I haven't decided yet. Long enough to teach him a lesson, but not so long that it discourages him."

"How do you know when that is? Is there a formula?" She wondered if he noticed the mocking sarcasm in her voice.

He picked up his glass and studied the juice that half filled it. "No, Anita, there's no formula, no equation or theorem that I invoke. I have to use my best judgment, my instincts about what is best for my son. Sometimes I'll be wrong. All I can do is pray that I don't make any big mistakes and hope he'll forgive me for the small ones." He replaced the glass on the end table without drinking, his eyes not leaving hers. "Please don't you be mad at me, too."

She relaxed into a smile. "I'm not mad at you, Jim. I'm just trying to understand, trying to put myself in his place."

"And I love you for that."

Love? Had he just said he loved her? Surely he didn't mean it the way it sounded.

"I have to get going," she said and rose from her chair.

If he realized she was retreating, withdrawing, he didn't say or do anything to show it.

"You won't get much sleep tonight," he said, halting her backward movement by slipping his arm around her waist and drawing her up against him.

Awareness of him and the time they had spent together before the phone call had her wanting to grin. As she gazed at his face, she also noted the tiny signs of fatigue around his eyes, at the corners of his mouth. He was a good man, a good dad. She wondered if she was being unreasonable in questioning the way he was dealing with his son's fighting.

"I liked the way the night started," she said.

A mischievous twinkle flashing in his dark eyes. "Me, too. Let's hope next time it ends better."

She let the words slosh around in her fuzzy brain. Yes, she wanted a next time very much. Better? She couldn't imagine it getting any better, but she was willing to let him prove her wrong.

"I like a challenge," she said.

The kiss that followed was long and passionate. He tried to lead her back to the couch.

"I really should be going," she protested. Too mildly, but Billy's bedroom was just at the head of the stairs, right across from his father's. They couldn't go up there again.

"Please don't leave yet," he begged. "Let me check on

Billy to make sure he's all right, then I have something important I want to talk to you about."

She felt exhausted, wrung out, but there was tantalizing excitement about the hushed way he invited her to stay. Besides, she'd much rather spend time with him than sleeping at home alone. If she could sleep at all. "Sure."

"I won't be long, I promise. You know where things are. Help yourself to anything you want in the bar, the fridge. I'll just be a minute."

"Don't worry about me."

He awarded her a quick kiss and dashed out of the room. She could hear him bounding up the stairs. What did he want to talk to her about? Her mind refused to settle on a subject.

Restless, edgy, she prowled the room. It had more of a lived-in look now with Jim and his son there. Billy's video game had been tossed on one of the leather chairs, along with his NASCAR cap. A couple of books had been pulled from the shelves and were sitting, one of them open, on a side table. The usually pristine desktop now had papers and folders on it, albeit in orderly piles. A legal-size yellow pad, set squarely in the middle. She went over to idly indulge her curiosity. The name *Taney* and *35M* were penciled on it in what she now recognized as Jim's distinctive script.

What did it mean? She'd seen the name scratched on a notepad by the telephone once before and had dismissed it as nothing more than one owner inquiring about another's health.

Thirty-five million? Dollars? Was that what Jim was asking for the team, or was it what Gideon Taney was offering for it? PDQ was worth at least that, probably more.

As she stared at the notation, sadness rippled through her. So Jim *was* going to sell PDQ. Richard would be horrified. She was horrified. It wasn't that she had anything against Taney, but she expected greater loyalty, more effort from Jim.

She heard the distant flush of a toilet, then the sound of him coming down the stairs. Like a guilty voyeur caught in the act of looking at something shameful, she migrated out from behind the desk and stood staring blindly at the big globe in the corner.

"How is he?" she asked, twirling it slowly with shaky fingers.

He came up beside her. "Cradled in the arms of Morpheus. I'm always amazed at how easily kids can fall asleep."

She almost said, "The innocence of youth." Instead, she asked, "What did you want to talk to me about, Jim?"

He took her extended hand and pressed it between his. "Sit with me awhile."

Uneasiness in his voice made her look over at him. She saw consternation in his features. Was this about PDQ? Was he about to tell her he was selling it after all?

They sat next to each other on the sofa. He turned toward her, his hands still clasping hers, as though he needed them for support.

"Anita," he began slowly, uncertainly, "something's happened since I met you, something I didn't expect to happen." He paused and held her gaze. "Anita, I've fallen in love with you."

Suddenly she felt lightheaded, dizzy. She opened her mouth, but before she could speak, he brought a hand up and touched his index finger to her lips. "Don't say anything. Not yet. Just let me tell you what you've come to mean to me."

She began to tremble. Did he feel it? Did he know he

was frightening her? No man had ever said those words to her before.

I've fallen in love with you.

What did he mean? Oh, she knew what the words were supposed to mean. For one thing, she'd fallen in love with him. Maybe not the soft sound of violins in the moonlight type of romantic love, although she felt that, too. But an emotion that was more than hearts and flowers. That special kind of relationship between two mature people.

"We complement each other," he said, "you and I. You fill a void in me that I didn't think anyone could ever fill. I'm not talking about Lisa. What I had with her was wonderful. I don't ever want to forget her and I doubt I ever will, but what you bring to me is something completely different, completely new. Lisa brought me what I needed then. You… You bring me what I need now."

And what was that? She wanted to ask, but before she had a chance, he released her hands and stood up. "I'm saying this all wrong." There was a note of frustration and anxiety in his tone.

He paced across the carpet, then came back and sat beside her again, though this time he didn't take her hands in his as he had the first time.

Why was he making such a production out of all this? He obviously wanted them to be more than friends, more than close friends. She did, too. Was he worried about what it would do to their professional relationship? That was a legitimate consideration, but they would be able to handle it, or at least try to. He was stirring her up inside. Where this passion might lead scared her. A long-term commitment? A permanent part in a family?

He had no idea how much she'd daydreamed about the time they'd spent together, how much she fantasized about exploring more of what he had made her feel. All those years of solitude, of wondering what it would be like to have someone—a man—to turn to, to love and be loved in return.

"I'm glad we're finally getting along so well." She gave him a thin smile. "It certainly didn't look very promising when we first met."

"When you bumped into me," he said lightly.

"Because you were crowding me," she pointed out.

"Did I ever tell you I was sorry? If I did, I was lying. I'm not sorry you bumped into me at all. I wasn't planning for us to meet that way, but I'm glad we did. I liked the feel of your body coming in contact with mine. Still do, and I want to make it happen more often."

She studied the curve of his lips. This flippant exchange would have eased the tension in her stomach another notch but for the way he was smiling at her, a knowing grin that sent little funnel clouds swirling inside her.

She placed a hand on top of his and squeezed. He turned it over and held it. Not forcefully, but firmly. His grip on her was possessive, supportive, yet surprisingly gentle. For a fractional moment, the strength of his hold was so alluring it made her want to curl up in it.

His voice when he finally spoke was even more mesmeric—more intimate—than when they had been beside each other in bed after the most beautiful experience she could ever imagine.

"Will you marry me?" he asked.

Her heart stopped, ached with shock, then resumed beating in even more painful thuds. Surely she'd misunderstood him. "What?"

"Will you marry me, Anita? Be my wife, a mother to my son, a mother to the children I want to have with you. Will you make me the happiest man in the world, Anita? Will you marry me?"

She stared at him, her pulse throbbing at double time. Flags were waving. They should be checkered flags, shouldn't they? Wasn't marriage the romantic equivalent of Victory Lane? But what she saw were big yellow caution flags. Danger. Hit the brakes. Slow the pace. Steer clear of obstacles.

She could feel his eyes burning into hers. Waiting. Begging. Pleading. But she didn't know what to say. He'd just said the words she'd longed to hear.

I love you. I want to marry you.

She loved him. She wanted to marry him. Yet… Her heart was pounding in her ears, thudding painfully in her chest. Her skin tingled. Sweat was breaking out at the same time she felt cold.

Will you marry me?

She always thought she'd know the answer to that question if it were ever asked. She'd always taken for granted that someday she'd get married, settle down and have kids. She'd never expected fear and trepidation to overpower the pure joy that battled its way through her. Or that fear would win. She was afraid—afraid to say yes, but unwilling to say no. Head bowed, she turned away from him. Maybe if the sight of him wasn't dominating her vision, filling her world it would be easier to find the words, to corral the emotions racing through her.

"Anita?" he asked in bafflement. "Did you hear me?"

CHAPTER TWENTY-FOUR

HER MOUTH WAS DRY. "I…heard you. I…I need time to think."

He placed his hands on her shoulders, and rotated her around to face him, then raised her chin with the side of his forefinger. There was gentleness in his touch, tenderness, but she couldn't avoid the confusion, the haunting bewilderment in his magically dark, shadowy eyes. He normally kept his emotions so well-guarded that she often found him indecipherable, inscrutable. Not this time. He was perplexed by her silence, stunned that she wasn't ready with an answer, worried she was about to say no. Above all, she saw the pain of rejection, the hurt of not being wanted. She would never have imagined that this man who was so strong, physically and emotionally, could be so vulnerable.

"Anita, what's the matter?" he asked softly.

She bit her lip. "We have a lot of issues separating us."

"We have a lot pulling us together, too."

"You don't like what I do for a living. You don't respect my line of work."

"I respect you, and I'm coming to appreciate how well you handle your job. We make a good team."

"You want to sell the team. I saw your note about Taney on your desk"

She saw the flash of anger that she had been spying on him, but it disappeared as his eyes searched hers. "No, I don't want to," he said, "but I will if I conclude I'm incompetent at running it. It wouldn't be fair to all the people who work so hard at making it a success for me to hang onto it for sentimental reasons. You wouldn't respect me if I did that."

He was right. Sometimes it took more strength to let go than to hold on. Maybe that was what she had to do—let him go—because she wasn't suited to the role he was casting her into.

"You're not only asking me to be your wife, Jim. There's Billy. I don't think I'm ready to be a stepmom."

She saw the muscles around his mouth relax slightly, as if he were finally beginning to understand.

"We're not as far apart as you seem to think, sweetheart. We agree on fundamentals, like the need for discipline. The details we can work out between us."

"Your idea of parenting is so completely different than mine."

"We're two different people. I hate to admit this, but we're never going to see eye to eye on everything, sweetheart. So what? We agree on the most important thing. I love…" He hesitated, and she saw the tension return. He backed away. "You don't love me. Is that it?"

How could she explain that love wasn't the issue? She had no doubt he was sincere in his protestation of love, and she knew in her heart that she loved him. But… "It isn't as easy as that."

"You're wrong," he told her, his voice even, resigned. "It's the only thing that is easy."

"I need time to think," she repeated and started gathering her things. Her hands shook. Her legs felt wobbly. He didn't offer to help her, didn't accompany her to the door.

She left him standing in the middle of the den, surrounded by awards and trophies and pictures of the past.

She went home. Except it wasn't her home anymore. Home was where the heart was, and she'd left hers with Jim Latimer, whether she had intended to or not. The house where she had grown up, where she'd cared for her chronically ill mother for so many years, where all her worldly goods were, wasn't a home anymore. It was just the place where she lived and where sleep eluded her.

She crawled out of bed at six o'clock the next morning, showered and dressed, prepared coffee, extra-strong, sat and tried to read the morning paper. But her mind couldn't stay focused.

Facts and information percolated into her brain, available for later retrieval, but they left no impression.

Another reported sighting of Hilton Branch. Ho-hum.

A feature article in the sports section offering analysis of the Branch brothers' records in NASCAR, along with speculation about whether they had a chance to make the Chase for the NASCAR Sprint Cup. Sigh.

A report that PDQ's chief sponsor was having second thoughts about backing Bart Branch because of his poor season performance and his family's continuing scandal and the many criminal and civil charges being leveled against them. Old news.

Except that this article was trying to tie Jim's father's criminal background to the possible demise of the racing team.

Bull.

This was just the type of vicious, groundless speculation Jim had complained about and that continued to keep him press-wary.

She finished her coffee, put the cup in the sink, grabbed her handbag and attaché case and headed for the office. Maybe there she'd find the inspiration and the energy to fight the latest slanderous assault on the integrity of two honorable men.

BILLY SLEPT LATE the following morning. Jim figured he needed the extra rest after the traumatic events of the previous night.

"You hungry?" he asked, when the boy came into the kitchen around 10:30.

He rubbed his eyes. "Yeah. Yes, sir," he corrected himself.

"There's your regular cereal, or I can fix you something hot."

"Will you make a Western omelet, Dad? We haven't had one of those in a long time."

Jim had to keep from grinning. Was the boy trying to butter him up? It really wasn't a bad tactic, even though it wouldn't yield the result he was probably hoping for.

"I think we have the makings," he said, "if you'll help me cut things up."

Billy snickered. "I'll do the green pepper and ham. You can do the onion."

Jim laughed. "Deal."

They set to work. Ten minutes latter the room was filled with the tantalizing aroma of sautéed vegetables, simmering eggs and toasting English muffins.

Jim cut the large, single omelet in two and placed equal portions on china plates which Billy took to the table by the window overlooking the back of the house and the glistening pool. Jim tried not to think about Anita in her skimpy bikini, splashing around in the water, laughing. Even when she wasn't there she drove him to distraction.

He had hoped he'd be able to tell his son this morning that he was getting a new mom, a stepmother. How would the boy react? Favorably, he thought, hoped. Happily. But that prospect seemed more and more remote as time went by without hearing from her. It had been eight hours now since he'd asked her to be his wife. Eight hours and thirty-two minutes without a word.

"Dad, I'm sorry about last night," Billy said after wolfing down the first few bites.

"I know you are, son."

"When are you going to let me take driving lessons again?"

"When do you think I should?"

"Tomorrow?" Tomorrow was Wednesday, his regular day at the training track.

Jim looked over and smiled. "Nice try."

Billy shrugged. He knew it wasn't going to happen. "Next week?"

"Is that going to give you enough time to understand what you did wrong."

"I know now."

"Yes, I suppose you do. Okay, next week."

Billy let out a huge sigh. "Thanks, Dad."

"You're welcome. You know, of course, that if it happens again—"

"It won't, Dad. I promise."

"MARRIAGE?" KYLIE'S FACE GLOWED with approval. "Oh that's wonderful. I'm so happy for you, Anita. Of course you'll have to train him to pick up his socks—"

"He doesn't leave them around."

She laughed and broke off a piece of her chocolate éclair with the side of her fork. "No, I don't suppose he does. Well, that's one hurdle you won't have to overcome. You can change the little things—well, some of them—just don't try to change who he is."

"Why would I want to do that?"

Kylie studied her friend's face more closely. "Uh-oh." They were sitting in a pastry shop not far from the office, a favorite refuge when they were in need of girl talk and chocolate. "Do I detect trouble in paradise already? Is that why you haven't answered yet?"

Anita toyed with the generous chunk of her rich Black Forest cherry cake. "You said not to try to change who he is. But how do I even know who he is?"

Kylie continued to scrutinize her friend. Pre-marriage jitters? That was certainly understandable, especially in this case. For all her outgoing sociability, Anita had lived a very sheltered life. She'd told Kylie she'd rarely dated, had never gone steady. For a thirty-year-old woman who'd had so little experience with men, the prospect of spending a lifetime with one—even one as adoring and adorable as Jim Latimer—must be daunting and downright scary.

"There's an easy answer to that," she said, reaching across the table and squeezing her friend's hand. "But it's not very helpful, I'm afraid. You already know. Deep down inside, Anita, you know." She sat back. "You know if you feel safe with him, if you trust him to honor and respect you. You know if you share the same values. Not necessarily the same tastes—though that certainly helps—but the same values. Do you?"

"I'm not sure," Anita mumbled. "Our tastes aren't all that different, but our values?" She shrugged.

Kylie put her fork down. She wasn't about to abandon that yummy cream-filled pastry, but for the moment it could wait. "What's really bothering you, girl?"

Anita toyed with her equally rich chocolate cake. "For one thing, there's the way he disciplines his son."

"You're referring to how he handled Billy's fights."

Anita nodded. "I know they're only two incidents and probably pretty minor ones, but they seem important to me. If we can't agree on how to handle them, how are we going to agree on the big issues?"

She was right on both counts. They were minor incidents in the overall scheme of things, yet they were important.

"Like where to live and whether to support Billy in his ambition to become a race car driver," she said half in jest, but her friend didn't seem to notice.

"I'm not being asked just to be a wife, Kylie. I'm being asked to be a mother to an eleven-year-old boy. I have no experience as a parent, much less of a boy, who in a couple of years will be a teenager, an adolescent."

It wasn't a phase of parenting Kylie was especially looking forward to, either. "Do you think Jim's a bad parent?"

"Of course not."

"Boys fight, honey. That's just the way they are. Actually, from all I've observed, Billy's a pretty good kid, especially considering what he's been through, losing his mother."

"I know. It's just that—"

"You would have handled the incidents differently."

Anita nodded.

"That's natural. My late husband and I didn't always agree, either, especially since Ben was a cop. He saw the world a lot differently than I do. Sometimes, I still ask myself how he would handle things."

"Does it change the way you deal with them as a result?"

Kylie chuckled. "Not really. Mostly, I just wish he were here to handle them for me."

"It must be tough."

Kylie nodded. "It gets easier with time. But yeah, it's tough."

They remained quiet for several minutes.

"Like I said, only you can decide." Kylie picked up her fork again and scooped up another hunk of the éclair. "You know in your heart what the answer is. It's up to you now to follow it."

CHAPTER TWENTY-FIVE

CHARLOTTE DAILY HERALD
NASCAR Drivers suspended and fined
Daytona Beach, FL—NASCAR officials announced Tuesday afternoon their decision regarding the incident in the garage area here Sunday in which Clyde Coogle attacked Bart Branch after the two drivers were involved in a pileup on the track that resulted in both their cars being eliminated from the race. Coogle, driver of the No. 452 car, received a one-race suspension and a fifty-thousand-dollar fine. Branch, driver of car No. 475, received the same fifty-thousand-dollar fine but was not suspended. When asked about the disparity in penalties, officials noted that Coogle initiated the battle of the fists, while Branch was only reacting. Branch, who drives for PDQ Racing, is currently in nineteenth place in the NASCAR Sprint Cup Series and more than 800 points behind the leader. Not being suspended means he still has a fighting chance to make the cut for the Chase for the NASCAR Sprint Cup. Because of Coogle's low point score—currently fifteen hundred points behind the leader—the suspension essentially eliminates him from the competition for the NASCAR Sprint Cup Series championship.

JIM USED THE PERSONAL telephone call he received from NASCAR officials informing him that Bart was being fined but not suspended as an excuse to call Anita. As if he needed one. He'd asked her to marry him last night. He'd sent flowers to her office this morning. Still, he hadn't heard a word from her. No phone call. No e-mail.

Which could mean only one thing. She was rejecting his proposal of marriage. Why? Didn't she love him? Did she not believe he loved her? Love wasn't a word he threw around lightly. He thought she understood that. Before he asked her to be his wife he'd told her he loved her. Maybe not strongly enough. Maybe he should have counted the ways. And he probably shouldn't have mentioned Lisa. But that wouldn't have been honest. He wasn't going to forget the mother of his son. He didn't want to. That didn't mean he couldn't get past her death, that he couldn't go on living as a man. Everything he'd told Anita was true, that she brought something to his life that he thought was gone. Feelings. Didn't women want men to talk about their feelings? How was a guy to know when it was okay and when it wasn't?

All he knew was that, at the moment, he was feeling confused and miserably lonely.

He received no answer on her home number. Out somewhere probably. He dialed her cell.

She picked up on the second ring.

"Hello, Jim." She didn't seem overjoyed to have him on the line. "I was getting ready to call you."

"Oh? About what?" he asked, hoping, in spite of her sad tone, it might be good news.

"You first," she said, and he knew she was putting off telling him what she had to say. Another bad sign.

"I just got a call from NASCAR. They're hitting Bart with a fifty-thousand-dollar fine but no suspension."

"That's good news." But she didn't sound as if it made much difference to her.

"Coogle got the same fine and a one-race suspension."

"That puts him out of the running then," she said. "He was on the edge point-wise anyway. No way he can make up the deficit now."

"And Bart is still in the game."

"Looks like Richard was right."

Jim chuckled softly. "I should have known better than to doubt him."

"Nobody knows the sport like he does."

All of a sudden they'd run out of small talk, and the line went quiet.

"What were you going to call me about?" he finally worked up the courage to ask.

He heard her take a breath before she said, "We need to get together…and talk."

"Come on over to my place this evening."

"Is there somewhere else we can meet? Without Billy?" she added.

Jim paused. "I'm sure if I ask Kylie she'll take him for a couple of hours, unless," he added hopefully, "you think he should spend the night. I don't think Kylie will mind, especially after I laid down the law with Billy."

"No," she said. "Just for a couple of hours. Maybe for dinner."

This was sounding worse and worse.

"Okay. Where do you want to meet?" he asked. "How about Chez Wolski?"

"I was thinking more along the lines of grabbing a sandwich or something and taking it to the park."

"We've never done a picnic before. Might be fun." Though he was well aware that she wasn't thinking of a picnic at all.

They settled on a time and place to meet, and he ended the call.

THEY MET BY THE POND in the park. He brought their dinners, two white paper bags with thick sandwiches, coarse crispy sourdough rolls, crammed with meat and vegetables, dressing on the side, and two medium-size non-carbonated drinks.

"You don't look like you got any more sleep last night than I did," he commented, as he handed over her dinner. No white linen. No wait staff hovering. No premium wine to sip.

"So much for the camouflage of makeup," she quipped.

"You're not wearing makeup," he said. She rarely did and then it was only lightly applied.

"No, but it sounds like I should be."

"I wasn't trying to offend you, Anita."

"I know, silly." She smiled wanly. "I'm teasing."

They spread their food out on the concrete table and sat across from each other in the shade of a sprawling oak tree. They took bites of their food, sipped their drinks, ate a little more, all in the kind of silence that was guaranteed to give indigestion.

Finally he couldn't take it any longer. He put down his sandwich, hardly a quarter eaten, pushed it toward the middle of the table and wished the seat had a back rest.

"Why?" he asked.

"Why what?" As if she didn't know.

"Why won't you marry me?" He was hoping desperately she would contradict him, tell him he had it all wrong, that she was happy and thrilled to accept his proposal, that she wanted to know how soon they could tie the knot. But he saw none of those reactions in her posture, in her eyes.

"I care about you, and I care about Billy. Very much." She put her food down, as well. "But it won't work, Jim."

"How can you say that?"

"Because it's true. I'm not prepared to take on the role of mother to an eleven-year-old boy. You're a good father, an excellent father. Billy is a very lucky kid to have a dad like you. But…"

He wanted so much to touch her. He needed to feel her skin, the smooth warmth of her flesh in contact with his. He rose to his feet, came around the end of the table and put his hands on her shoulders. They were rigid, tight. He gently squeezed, massaged, hoping to relieve some of the tension. But even as he worked her taut muscles, he felt no give, no relaxation. She was determined, adamant, obstinate. Breaking his heart.

"Why do you think we can't be good parents together? I think we make a very good team."

She rocked her head from side to side in denial. "That's the thing. You approach situations and see one thing. I see another."

He sat down beside her, his feet on the outside of the bench, hers on the inside, so that their thighs touched as they faced each other.

"That's perfectly natural, sweetheart. As much as I hope to share my life with you, as much as I want us to be one, I recognize we're two separate people. That's healthy. That's the way it should be. Two separate people united. Of course we're going to bring different perspectives to some situations. I'm a man and you're a woman. We'll never see things quite the same way. Sometimes I'll be right. Sometimes you will be, and sometimes, probably most of the time, the answer will lie somewhere between us. It's called compromise, a meeting of the minds."

He could see by her somber, downcast expression, her clasped hands that he wasn't getting through, wasn't convincing her.

"We don't disagree on fundamentals," he reminded her. "We differ sometimes on the means to achieve them, but our goals are the same. That's the important thing."

"It isn't enough," she muttered. "I agree with everything you've said, but I don't have the skills it takes to be a good stepmother to an eleven-year-old boy. I just don't. I'm sorry."

She struggled to get to her feet. He didn't move away to give her room to extricate her legs from under the table. He was hoping she would put her hand on his shoulder, so he could take advantage of the contact, but she pivoted away from him.

"Where have things gone so wrong?" he asked, looking up at her.

She kept her rigid back to him. "I'm not sure they were ever right," she said, still without facing him. "We just wanted them to be."

"You're wrong." He stood up, too, but only by force of will was he able to maintain his distance from her. "What I feel for you isn't illusion, and I don't believe what you feel for me is simply wishful thinking. I understand what love is, Anita. I've known it. I've experienced it, and I know what I feel for you is not just the attraction of a male to a female. If I could never touch you again, I would still love you."

She turned to him now, her eyes wet with tears. "Don't say that. I don't doubt the sincerity of your words, but what you think you're feeling now is only temporary."

"You're not making sense. You know that, don't you? One minute you're afraid because you don't know how to handle our relationship, the next you're an expert on what will and what won't work. Make up your mind."

She covered her tear-stained face with her hands.

He moved closer, gently pulled her hands away and tipped her head up to meet his eyes.

"What are we going to do now, Anita?"

She refused to maintain eye contact with him. "I don't know," she murmured.

"It can't be business as usual, you know. I can't walk into a room and treat the woman I love, the woman I've made love to… I can't treat her like she's no more than an acquaintance, a professional colleague."

"If you sell the team," she ventured, "we won't have to see each other anymore."

"I never said I was going to sell the team," he flared. "And even if I did, it wouldn't be for months. What are we supposed to do in the meantime?"

She nodded without raising her head. "I'll talk to Sandra, ask her to assign someone else to represent Bart. Maybe Kylie and I can trade clients."

"You think that's the solution? That we simply walk around

each other? I can't do that, Anita. I've fallen in love with you. Don't you understand that? Whether you're willing to accept my love or not, I love you. I can't just turn it off, like a spigot or a light switch. What am I going to do without you?"

She shook her head wildly and turned away from him. Again.

"And what about Billy?" he called out. "You've filled a gap in his life, too. Can you just abandon him?"

"Why are you doing this?" She spun around in a fury. "Why are you putting this guilt trip on me?"

He looked at her directly and hard. "Because I want you to tell me you don't love me. Say it, Anita. Say, 'I don't love you, Jim.'"

Her features stiffened.

"You can't, can you? You can't say those simple words that will end this once and for all. Say them, Anita. Tell me you don't love me."

She hiccoughed, then said in a quavering voice, "I don't love you, Jim."

His jaw tightened as he stared at her. "I don't know which is harder," he said in a low murmur, "believing you or not believing you."

CHAPTER TWENTY-SIX

WHATEVER IT WAS SHE MAY have done Tuesday evening and through that night, Anita had no recollection of it. She was fairly certain she hadn't eaten anything after leaving Jim at the park, because the next day she was ravenous, though she had no appetite. She knew she had driven home only because she was there and her car was in the garage, without any scratches or crumpled fenders, as far as she could tell.

Jim Latimer, a man with whom she had spent more time than with any man in her memory, the only man who had ever told her he loved her, had asked her to marry him, and she had said no. Even now, with him expelled from her life, she wished he were there with her so she could ask him, as a friend, if she had done the right thing. Her mind said she had, but her heart…well, her heart was a different matter.

At work on Wednesday she was tempted to walk into Sandra's office—or Kylie's—and close the door, talk and cry, cry and talk. She needed to do both, but she couldn't bring herself to do either. So she kept busy in other ways, procrastinated, set about doing all the things she had to do before a race weekend. She sent out press releases, reviewed Bart's appearance schedule, arranged press conferences, worked out different approaches to the stories that might develop—if Bart won the race in Chicago; if he did well but didn't win; if his performance was mediocre, and he finished in the middle of the pack; if he didn't finish at all. There was always an angle to be spun. No matter how things turned out, she would find a way to give it a smiley face. Even when she didn't feel like smiling. Isn't that what a professional did, make it look easy?

She wasn't scheduled to fly to Chicago until Friday morning, in time to catch qualifying laps that afternoon, so in her office on Thursday she was going over the program of events, trying to get into the zone for the coming weekend, when the phone rang.

She checked the caller ID. Jim.

She felt a familiar flutter in her chest, followed by a pang of regret. He was probably just confirming something on the schedule. He could have done it by e-mail. The thought of hearing his voice raised her spirit, while the realization that she would have to respond without giving away what she felt in her heart plunged her into depression.

She lifted the receiver. "Hello, Jim."

"Anita." He paused, and for a moment she was afraid the line had gone dead, or he had disconnected. "I'm calling about Richard. He's had another stroke."

Her heart sank. "Oh, no. How bad? Where are you?"

"At the hospital. I'm sorry to impose on you, but would it be possible for you to pick up Billy for me? He's at his friend Eddie Farrell's house, but I really don't want to leave here to get him, just in case—"

"Of course. Do you want me to bring him there?"

"I hate to impose."

"Give me the name and address."

He did. "I'll call Leslie Farrell and tell her you're coming to get him."

"Does he know yet?" she asked.

"No, I—"

"Good. Tell Leslie I'm on my way but that she shouldn't say anything to Billy. I'll break the news when I pick him up."

"Thank you, Anita. I'm sorry—"

"What about Richard? What do the doctors say?"

"They don't think he's going to make it this time."

"I'm sorry, Jim."

"Yeah, me, too." There was a pause. "Just get Billy for me."

"We won't be long."

She went to Sandra's office and explained what was going on.

"Kylie isn't in," Anita said. "I'm not sure where she is. I haven't tried her cell phone yet. I'm hoping she might be able to pitch in for me in Chicago. I know it's irregular, since Bart isn't her client and is technically in competition with hers—" She was rambling.

Sandra waved her concerns aside. "I'll make sure Bart gets taken care of. I'll go myself, fly up with Taney. It will be fun. Don't worry about it."

"Thanks, and I'm sorry, but Richard feels like family to me."

"Take care of the rest of that family, Anita. They're going to need you. Now get out of here."

The Farrells lived just north of Charlotte. It took her about twenty minutes in mid-day traffic to get there. She rang the doorbell.

Leslie must have been watching, because she opened the

door almost immediately. She was a big woman with a lovely smooth complexion, dark hair and alert brown eyes. Introductions didn't take more than a few seconds.

"Jim called and told me. I'm so sorry. I haven't said anything to Billy. He doesn't know you're coming. They're out at the pool."

She led Anita through a large, comfortable house with high ceilings and chintz-covered furniture to a set of sliding glass doors. Beyond the fieldstone patio was a rectangular pool. Half a dozen kids, ranging from Billy's size to a couple of strapping teenagers who appeared big enough to be high school quarterbacks, were clowning around with a ball that must have been three feet in diameter.

Anita stepped outside ahead of her hostess. It took a minute before Billy looked up and noticed her, then he froze in place.

"Hi." He was understandably confused. "What are you doing here? Did Dad bring you?"

"No," she said, her belly quivering. "He called me and asked me to come by and pick you up."

"How come?" He was leery.

"Why don't you get dressed, and I'll tell you."

"You're leaving already?" one of the other kids asked. "You were supposed to stay for supper."

"I'm sorry," Anita started to explain, "But he has to—"

"Eddie, mind your manners," Leslie ordered him. "You go on playing. I'll explain to you later."

"Something's wrong, isn't it?" Billy challenged as he mounted the ladder and stepped onto the cool deck. "Has something happened to Dad?"

"Your dad is fine. He just wanted me to come and pick you up."

"Something's happened to him. I know it. I can tell by the way you're looking at me. Something's happened to Dad."

"I promise you," Anita said. "Your dad is fine. Really."

He absently accepted the towel Leslie handed him and started drying himself off. "Where is he?"

There was no easy way to say this, Anita realized, and perhaps telling him here was better than in the car.

"He's at the hospital, Billy. Uncle Richard has had another stroke. He's very sick."

The boy's eyes went wide. "Is he dead?"

"He wasn't when your dad called me a little while ago."

"But he's going to die, isn't he? Just like Mom," he shouted. "He's going to die."

Everyone stopped what they were doing and stared at him.

"He might, Billy," Anita said quietly. "I honestly don't know. I'd tell you if I did. All I know is that he's in very serious condition, the doctors are worried about him, and your dad needs you."

Leslie came up to them. "Your clothes are in Eddie's room, Billy," she said with kindness in her voice. "Go change. I'll put some of your favorite cookies in a bag so you can take them with you."

Billy ran off, uncertain, unhappy and scared. Anita understood why. Life seemed so unfair.

He was back in less than three minutes. His hair was cut short enough that he didn't need to comb it, but it was still damp.

Leslie walked them through the house to the front entrance. In the driveway, she held the car door for the boy and closed it after him, while Anita started the engine, then she waved as they pulled out into the street.

On the drive to the hospital, Anita tried to figure out what to say to Billy.

"Dad told me you probably wouldn't be coming around anymore," he said. "Are you mad at me, too?"

"I'm not mad at you, Billy, and I don't think your dad is, either. I'm just very busy with NASCAR and Bart Branch right now."

"You're lying. That's not the reason."

The uninhibited boldness of his statement shook her. Even more, it hurt, because it was true. How could she explain to him that she wouldn't be coming around anymore because his father had asked her to marry him, to be the boy's stepmom, and that the notion was so terrifying she was running away from him, too. First his mom died, now his beloved uncle was dying, and Anita was abandoning him.

They arrived in silence at the main entrance of the medical complex. Richard wouldn't be in the rehab center now, so Anita approached the woman at the receptionist's desk and asked for his room number.

This time at the nurses' station on the sixth floor she turned right instead of left and proceeded down an unfamiliar corridor.

Jim was sitting on a hard wooden bench in the hallway when they turned the corner. Billy ran to him and threw his arms around him.

Jim hugged his shoulders, then looked beyond him to Anita. She saw sadness, pain and regret in his dark eyes.

"Thank you for bringing him," he said, his voice gravelly.

She dismissed the remark with an impatient shake of her head. "How is he?"

"There's no brain activity. They're just waiting for my permission to—"

Pull the plug. He didn't have to say the words.

"Permission to what, Dad?" Billy had by then broken away and was looking up at his father. "Do they have to do an operation?"

Jim rubbed his forehead. There was no easy way to explain this. "Uncle Richard's brain has stopped functioning, Billy. His heart is beating only because there is a machine telling it to."

"But the machine is going to help him get better, right?"

"I'm afraid not, son. As soon as they turn it off, his heart will stop beating, too."

"But they can't. They can't turn it off. He'll get better. I know he won't be able to walk anymore. He told me. So I'll push him around in his wheelchair. I don't mind. And I'll help him learn to talk again, too."

"He's not going to get better this time. It's time for us to say goodbye and let him go."

"No-o-o." He began to beat with the heels of his fists against his father's chest. "You can't turn off the machine. You can't let him die. Not him, too."

Jim let him pound. Anita knew the tears welling up in his eyes were not from the blows. After a minute he took hold of the boy's wrists and gently contained the rage.

Billy tore out of his father's grasp and bolted over to Anita. "Don't let him do it. Please. Don't let him."

Her gaze settled on Jim. He looked at her helplessly.

She ushered Billy over to the wooden bench. "Let's sit down and talk." It was every bit as uncomfortable as it looked, but that didn't matter. She placed the boy between his father and her, swiveled around to face him and took his hand.

"What's the favorite thing you remember about your mom?" she asked, ignoring Jim's arched eyebrows, but very much aware of him gazing at her.

The boy looked at her funny for a minute. "Helping her in the garden." He grew pensive for a moment, then he grinned. "She always laughed if I sprayed her with the hose by mistake when she asked me to water the things she had just planted. She never got mad or anything." He paused to think. "And the look on her face when she saw her flowers blooming. She had flowers all over the place, and she would teach me all their names."

He stopped and his face took on a melancholy expression, his eyes growing misty. "And I liked the way she smelled when she kissed me good night."

"And when you see flowers now you always think of her smile."

"Yeah."

"My father died when I was about your age. Know what makes me think of him?"

"No? What?"

"The smell of lumber. He was a carpenter, and when he came home at night and picked me up to whirl me around, he always smelled of cut wood. He laughed a lot, too, so when I smell lumber now I think of him, and I feel happy."

"Do you miss him?"

"Sure I do. Just like you miss your mom."

He nodded.

"What are your favorite memories of Uncle Richard?"

He didn't hesitate. "Banana splits and NASCAR races."

"Banana splits?"

"Whenever Uncle Richard came to visit us, he always

took us to a place in our town that serves malted milks and banana splits. I didn't like the malteds, but the banana splits are really good. Up in the suites at NASCAR races he always makes sure they serve banana splits, too. He said they reminded him of someone he knew a long time ago."

"Well, I'll be darned," she said and grinned. "I didn't know about that." Had Richard been referring to that long-lost love, the fiancée who died just before they were supposed to get married? Anita conjured up the image of a pretty girl in bobby socks and freckles sharing a banana split with him or each with a straw making eyes with each other, as they hovered over a frosty glass of malted milk at a drug store soda fountain. Definitely a Norman Rockwell moment.

"So you see you have good memories of your uncle. But now it's time to say goodbye. You get to keep the memories, but you have to let him go."

"But I don't want to," he moaned.

Anita lowered her head. "I don't want to, either, just like I didn't want to let my mom go, but I had to."

"Is she dead?"

"She died two years ago."

"Did she have a stroke, too?"

"She had a disease called multiple sclerosis, MS, and she had it for a long time, fifteen years. After a while she got very weak and she couldn't do anything for herself, and then she finally got so weak, she couldn't live anymore—" *and didn't want to* "—so I had to say goodbye to her."

"Did you have to turn off a machine?"

"No," she acknowledged. She had at least been spared that agony. "But I would have, if she had been brain dead like Uncle Richard."

"What are your favorite memories of your mom?" he asked.

"That's easy." Anita smiled. "Sewing. Before she got sick my mother used to sew wonderful things. I still have a dress at home that she made for me. It's pink and much too small for me to wear now and completely out of style, but I keep it anyway, just to remind me. And crocheting. She crocheted a tablecloth that I still have. It's like delicate lace. It took her a long time to make. If I ever use it, it will have to be a very special occasion, and it'll always remind me of her before she got sick."

She paused, as her own memories flooded her, but she didn't have the luxury of time to reminisce. Not now.

"It was time for my mother to die, Billy, so I had to let her go, and now it's time to let Uncle Richard go. It doesn't mean we don't love him or that we'll ever forget him. We'll always have our memories of him with us."

He nodded.

"You ready?" she asked, holding him at arm's length. "Let's go in and say goodbye to Uncle Richard."

They spent about fifteen minutes with the dying man, talking to him, though the likelihood of his hearing seemed doubtful. It wasn't easy, enunciating words through the lumps in their throats. Billy thanked him for all the fun they had had together—and for the banana splits—and said he still wanted to be a race car driver, and maybe someday he'd try a malted milk and like it.

A hospital official came in quietly and asked Jim to sign a form on a clipboard. He did. A minute later the heart-lung machine was turned off. Uncle Richard continued to breathe and his heart kept the little squiggle on the monitor beeping.

The doctor said that was normal, but that after a while it would stop.

Almost an hour went by. At first they waited in silence, then Anita got Billy talking about some of the places he had been with Uncle Richard, the different race tracks, the people they had met.

Billy was talking about the NASCAR Nationwide Series race in Bristol last year—Billy's first NASCAR experience—when the machine stopped beeping and made a constant high-pitched tone.

The doctor rushed in a few seconds later, used his stethoscope to examine his patient, then turned off the monitoring device.

"Is he dead?" Billy asked.

"I'm afraid so," the doctor told him.

The three of them, Jim, Billy and Anita, hugged each other in a circle.

CHAPTER TWENTY-SEVEN

JIM WAS KEPT BUSY OVER the next few days with funeral arrangements and memorial-service plans. Anita issued all the public statements, the announcement of Richard Latimer's death and his obituary; she arranged for press interviews with many of the people who had known him over the years.

"I know it seems predatory to you," she told Jim the morning after Richard's passing. She'd been up most of the night coordinating details. Being able to treat it as an event instead of an ordeal helped keep her functioning, and her mind off Jim and his son.

"It is," he replied. "But I also recognize it's necessary, and I'm very grateful to you for carrying the load. I wouldn't have known where to begin or how to do it on my own."

"Yeah," she said, a little cynically, "I make it look easy."

Bart came in third in Chicago on Sunday. Jim called him and congratulated him on a good race. He had watched it in fits and starts with Billy and Anita at Richard's house, on the huge wall-mounted screen in the den, where he was busy going through yet more papers. His uncle's estate, while carefully set up for the inevitability of his death, would still be a complicated affair. After all, the man had been a multimillionaire. He had provided generously for his sisters and brother—a trust fund was set up for the latter, with Jim as administrator. Charitable trusts and an education fund were well-endowed. The residual of his money and property went to Jim and Billy.

The funeral for Richard Latimer was conducted on Monday, after Chicago so that race people who wanted to attend could. Not many NASCAR personalities missed it, and those who did sent sincere apologies. Had Jim allowed all those who wanted to give eulogies to do so, the event would have lasted for days.

At the reception that followed, Jim was finally able to corner Anita and tell her he would like her to come to the house that evening, that they had one more matter that had to be taken care of.

It was after seven when she finally arrived. Jim had changed out of his coat and tie and met her at the door wearing comfortably worn jeans and a blue pullover. She was still in her dark pinstripe business suit.

"Did you bring something more comfortable to change into?" he asked.

"No," she said, clearly annoyed at the difference in their apparel. "I haven't been home yet."

"I was hoping we might sit outside by the pool, maybe go for a swim."

"If this was a social invitation, you should have told me. I could have come prepared—or not at all."

He gazed at her with amusement. She was irritable, which was understandable. She must be exhausted, given the level of energy she'd expended in the past few days. But he sensed defensiveness, too, and wondered why she felt she had to be afraid.

"You can at least remove your jacket, can't you?" he asked.

She shrugged, slipped it off, draped it over the back of the couch and sat down beside it. Looking up, she asked, "What did you want to talk to me about, Jim?"

He studied her from halfway across the room. "You told me once you weren't the enemy. Is that what I've become?"

Shaking her head and sighing, she wilted into the cushiony sofa. "Of course not. Chalk it up to fatigue. I haven't been sleeping very much the past few nights."

He went over to the wet bar, removed a bottle of chardonnay from the under-counter refrigerator, the cork already loosened, and poured two glasses. He brought them over and handed her one. She accepted it with thanks.

"Where's Billy?" she asked.

"He needed a break. This past week has been pretty intense for him. He's spending the night over at Ryan's house."

"It's been intense for all of us," she said, taking a sip of her wine. She looked tired and drawn. He wanted so much to fold her in his arms, feel the warmth of her body pressed against him and soothe away the ragged tension.

He sat at the other end of the couch, turned toward her, one leg folded on the seat beside him, and gazed at her. He allowed a long moment to elapse.

"Thanks for all your help. You've been incredible. I mean it. Seems like every time I thought of something that needed doing, you'd already taken care of it."

She smiled a little shyly. Compliments always seemed to

embarrass her. Humility was but one of her many endearing qualities. "Just doing my job."

He let the moment linger. "You're wrong, you know."

She lifted her gaze from the wine she'd been contemplating. "About my job?"

Why were they playing these word games? he wondered. Surely she knew what he meant, what was really going through his mind, how he felt.

"Thank you for helping Billy accept his great uncle's death… No one could have done it better."

She shrugged. "I've been there. I can understand what he's going through."

Jim deposited his wine glass on the coffee table and moved up beside her. He was near enough to touch her, but against every impulse writhing within him, he maintained that delicate gap of separation.

"I've dealt with death, too, Anita, but there is no way I could translate my feelings and emotions into the kind of sympathetic counseling you gave my son. You're better at it than I was when his mother died."

"You were too close to the situation. You probably needed somebody to help you grieve as much as Billy needed you."

"My point is that you don't seem to think you have parenting skills, but you do—skills that are sincere and heartfelt. You did what I couldn't do. You helped him accept a reality that is unpleasant but unavoidable, and you made him richer for the experience."

"I was lucky, that's all."

He grinned at her. "I don't think so." He tipped her chin up and slowly brought his lips to hers. He kissed her. Lightly. Affectionately. Teasingly.

"Did you mean it when you said you didn't love me?" he asked quietly a minute later.

She bowed her head. "No. The truth is I love you so much it hurts."

Emboldened, he wrapped his arms around her this time. When she returned the embrace, he felt a spike of pleasure so strong he was sure he was going to lose control then and there. He needed this woman. Couldn't she see that? He took her hands in his, as they sat half-turned to each other.

"What are you afraid of, Anita? Don't you know I would never hurt you?"

"I'm not afraid of you," she murmured. "I'm afraid of disappointing you and not being a good mother to Billy."

This, he realized, was the essence of the woman he loved and why he loved her. Selflessness. She focused all her energy on other people. It made him feel greedy and selfish for wanting her.

"You won't disappoint me," he assured her softly. "You never will. As for Billy, you fill a place in his heart that's been empty, a place a father can't fill. He loves you, sweetheart. He couldn't ask for a better stepmom."

She lowered her gaze. "What you say, Jim, overwhelms me, humbles me. You and Billy have shown me what it's like to be part of a family, and I am more grateful to both of you for that than you can ever know. But being a family isn't something to do on weekends or over dinner once a week. At least it shouldn't be, and it's not something to walk away from when we don't agree."

"No," he concurred, "it isn't."

"But you and I disagree on so many things," she protested. "How can we make a family when we're always arguing?"

"Why do we have to argue? Why can't we discuss our differences? We've learned to compromise and complement each other in business matters. Why can't we do the same with family matters, too? The way each of us handles discipline is sometimes going to be different. That's natural. I'm a man and you're a woman. I like to think I'm a good father, but a boy needs a good mother, too."

"I don't have the skill or the right," she protested.

"You do have the skills, sweetheart. That's what I've been trying to tell you. You're a natural. As for the right, I'm giving you the right. I don't want to do this alone, Anita. I want you by my side. I need you there, helping me, guiding me, guiding my son. He needs you."

"I love him, too," she whispered.

"And he loves you, almost as much as I do." He smiled reassuringly. "We can make it, Anita, you and me and Billy. We can make it, and the love we share will make us stronger, better people."

He framed her face gently with both his hands and felt the gentle tattoo of her pulse. "Let me ask you the question again—and I warn you, I'm going to keep asking it until you say yes—Anita, will you marry me?"

She bit her lips and smiled up at him through her tears.

"You drive a hard bargain, Jim Latimer." Her emerald-green eyes twinkled. "But since you put it that way—" she leaned forward and touched her lips to his "—I don't seem to have much of a choice. Yes, I'll marry you."

EPILOGUE

"I DON'T KNOW WHY I NEVER thought of Happy Home Dairy as a sponsor before," Anita said after sticking out her tongue and licking the spoon.

"Because you didn't know about the significance of banana splits," Jim reminded her.

She took another spoonful of ice cream as she stared out the huge picture window at the Indianapolis track below. "I knew there had to be a good reason."

"They're down to the last five laps," Billy excitedly announced a few feet away, though it wasn't necessary. Everyone in the suite was staring out the window.

Bart had run an incredible race. Starting off in the twenty-seventh position, he'd moved up steadily and was now in fourth place. Justin Murphy was in the lead by several car lengths, and unless something dramatic happened—like blowing an engine or losing a wheel—he was destined for Victory Lane.

In Jim's estimation that was just fine. Bart was doing well and in a good position to make the Chase. Not that it mattered; Jim had already made up his mind to keep him on, regardless of his final standing. A bonus was that Anita had identified a national dairy producer, who had just started marketing a banana-split ice cream, as a potential PDQ sponsor. Mark Jessup, the EZ-Plus Software VP, had shown lukewarm interest in continuing the software manufacturer's sponsorship of car No. 475 until he realized he had competition. Suddenly the ante had gone up.

"Uncle Richard would be proud of you," Jim told Anita.

"He'd be proud of you, too," she said, as the lead pack, down now to six cars, rounded the fourth turn and were given the white flag, signifying the last lap. "What did Taney say when you spoke to him?"

Jim had told her about Taney's offer to buy PDQ Racing and the serious consideration Jim had given to it back when Bart had been doing so poorly. This past Friday, while the drivers were running their qualifying laps, Taney had called to renew his offer. They'd met face-to-face that afternoon.

"He admitted he was disappointed," Jim replied, his eyes glued to the action on the track below, "but he said he understood. Then he surprised me by adding that I was doing the right thing. Said he looked forward to many years of competition between us."

She laughed. "I guess it was obvious even to him that NASCAR is in your blood."

Jim draped his arm around her shoulders. "Obvious to everyone but me."

It amazed him that he hadn't appreciated how much he'd grown to love the sport. Watching it as a fan had been fun. Getting involved in it as an owner had been terrifying and had distorted his outlook, just as seeing Anita as a member of the media—rather than as a person—had blinded him. There had never been any doubt about her being a woman. At least for a while. As with so many other things, Uncle Richard had had more insight into him than Jim. Like the stocks Jim had sold at a loss. They'd zoomed up in price this past week, more than doubling in value. He could imagine his uncle chuckling at his lack of faith.

"Some lessons we have to learn for ourselves," Anita said, smiling up into his eyes.

"Can I have some more?" Billy asked, holding out his empty ice cream dish.

"How many have you had already?" she asked him.

"Three," he admitted a bit sheepishly.

"I think that's enough. You don't want to get sick."

"Okay," he conceded fatalistically, then brightened. "Can I have more later?"

She ran her hand across the top of his head. "As long as later isn't before tomorrow."

He looked up at this father for relief, but Jim just quirked an eyebrow, indicating Anita had spoken.

The boy shrugged—it had been worth a try—then went to join his friends. Eddie was one of them. The Farrells were somewhere in the suite, intermingling with other guests. They'd been thrilled when Jim invited them to attend the race as his guests, and they'd been even more excited when he asked them to fly to the race with him and Billy on PDQ's private jet.

"Like being a parent," Jim whispered in Anita's ear. "You're a natural."

Their wedding would be at his family's home in Tennessee on the Saturday after Thanksgiving, following the end of the NASCAR Sprint Cup Series season. Both Jim and Anita would have liked to move it up, but his family had been adamant that they needed time to do it right. Billy was excited about being his dad's best man.

"Have I mentioned to you lately that I love you?" he asked, as they stood side by side, his arm around her waist, hers around his.

"Not since lap 110," she told him.

He bent his head down to whisper in her ear. "I love you."

"It's the red hair, right?"

"Yep," he said. "Among other things."

REQUEST YOUR FREE BOOKS!

2 FREE NOVELS PLUS 2 FREE GIFTS!

SPECIAL EDITION®

Life, Love and Family!

YES! Please send me 2 FREE Silhouette Special Edition® novels and my 2 FREE gifts (gifts are worth about $10). After receiving them, if I don't wish to receive any more books, I can return the shipping statement marked "cancel." If I don't cancel, I will receive 6 brand-new novels every month and be billed just $4.24 per book in the U.S. or $4.99 per book in Canada, plus 25¢ shipping and handling per book and applicable taxes, if any*. That's a savings of at least 15% off the cover price! I understand that accepting the 2 free books and gifts places me under no obligation to buy anything. I can always return a shipment and cancel at any time. Even if I never buy another book from Silhouette, the two free books and gifts are mine to keep forever.

235 SDN EEYU 335 SDN EEY6

Name	(PLEASE PRINT)	
Address		Apt. #
City	State/Prov.	Zip/Postal Code

Signature (if under 18, a parent or guardian must sign)

Mail to the **Silhouette Reader Service:**

IN U.S.A.: P.O. Box 1867, Buffalo, NY 14240-1867
IN CANADA: P.O. Box 609, Fort Erie, Ontario L2A 5X3

Not valid to current subscribers of Silhouette Special Edition books.

Want to try two free books from another line?
Call 1-800-873-8635 or visit www.morefreebooks.com.

* Terms and prices subject to change without notice. N.Y. residents add applicable sales tax. Canadian residents will be charged applicable provincial taxes and GST. Offer not valid in Quebec. This offer is limited to one order per household. All orders subject to approval. Credit or debit balances in a customer's account(s) may be offset by any other outstanding balance owed by or to the customer. Please allow 4 to 6 weeks for delivery. Offer available while quantities last.

Your Privacy: Silhouette is committed to protecting your privacy. Our Privacy Policy is available online at www.eHarlequin.com or upon request from the Reader Service. From time to time we make our lists of customers available to reputable third parties who may have a product or service of interest to you. If you would prefer we not share your name and address, please check here. ☐

SSE08R